MURDER BUYS A LEMON

CHRISTY FIFIELD

Christy Fifield

Cover Image © @julos via Deposit Photos

Cover Design © 2022 J. Steven York

Cover Template © 2022 Allyson Longueira

ISBN 978-1-946199-01-0 (digital)

ISBN 978-1-946199-03-4 (print)

❀ Created with Vellum

CHAPTER 1

Southern Treasures, my souvenir shop on the main street of Keyhole Bay, Florida, hummed with activity. Tourists browsed the shelves of knickknacks and souvenirs, a few stopping to inspect the vintage kitchenware, magazines, and newspapers that set my shop apart from the dozens of souvenir stores strung out along the Panhandle.

A couple paused at the back wall to admire the handmade—and expensive—quilts hung there.

At the counter my assistant, Julie, smiled and chatted and efficiently rang up sales. Julie was my treasure, a young local woman who'd come to work for me four years ago while still in her teens. She'd become an invaluable part of the operation, along with Chloe, who manages my recently-purchased coffee shop next door.

"Coffee?"

I turned and shook my head at Bluebeard, the parrot I'd inherited along with the store. I swear, sometimes I thought that bird could read my mind.

"No coffee," I scolded. "You know better. Coffee will make you

eard hung his head, putting on a show for the kids that clustered around his perch. He definitely knew how to play to a crowd. "Coffee?" he said in the saddest voice imaginable.

The children watched expectantly. I realized they all knew this game; they'd probably played it with their parents dozens, or hundreds, of times.

I sighed. There was no way I could give in to his demand for coffee; it really was toxic for parrots. But our audience was waiting to see what I would do.

So I caved. I might be setting a bad example, but I didn't think so. Compromise was a good thing, right?

"Biscuits," I said. "Not coffee."

Opening the can of shredded-wheat biscuits underneath his cage I offered one to each of the three kids. "Would you like to give him a treat?" I asked.

One little girl hesitated, but the other girl and the boy each snatched a biscuit from the tin and held them out.

Bluebeard, knowing when he had to accept a compromise, carefully took a biscuit and crunched it in his powerful beak. He could be extremely gentle when he wanted to, and seemed to have a soft spot for children.

Also for attractive women. Fortunately he knew when he could get away with his piercing wolf-whistle and when he couldn't. Like right now, while the shop was full of the tourists that kept our bills paid.

The bell over the front door rang, catching his attention, and mine. My best friend—and news reporter for local radio station WBBY— Karen Freed breezed in. With her auburn curls tied atop her head in a concession to the midsummer heat, she would have rated a whistle from Bluebeard if the store was empty.

Instead he contented himself with a whispered, "Pretty girl," and went back to take the second biscuit.

The second girl still didn't take a biscuit, and Bluebeard turned his attention back to Karen, who had crossed the shop to join me next to his perch.

She reached over and gave him a pat. "You do know how to flatter a girl, don't you?"

2

Bluebeard preened and repeated himself. "Pretty girl."

Karen smiled fondly. "You're pretty special yourself."

The kids took turns carefully petting the parrot but were soon retrieved by their parents. I noticed the Bluebeard T-shirts tucked into their shopping bags, one for each child. Those shirts had become one of our best sellers, and they'd been Julie's idea.

Like I said, she's a treasure.

Once the children were out of earshot, Bluebeard gave a very soft whistle. I shot him a stern look, but it only triggered a bout of muttered complaint as he stomped into his cage and turned his back on us.

"In a mood, are we?" Karen said to his back with a laugh.

More muttering floated out of the cage.

Karen chuckled before turning back to me. "So, how's the construction going?"

I glanced toward the ceiling and my apartment above the shop, then back at Karen. "The contractor and his crew showed up early and I came downstairs as soon as they did. They made a tremendous amount of noise and then knocked off early."

"Since then I've been kind of afraid to go up and see what they did."

She glanced up at the vintage cartoon-cat clock on my back wall. "I don't have to be back to the station for another twenty minutes," she said. "I was hoping you'd give me a tour. But it sounds like maybe I need to give *you* moral support to go check out the progress."

I shrugged. After I bought Lighthouse Coffee last winter, it had seemed like a good idea to open up my small apartment over the souvenir shop into the under-utilized space over the bakery/coffee shop. It took several months to put the plans into place, and I'd been excited to start the project.

Right up to the point where the contractor showed up with his crew and a truckload of power tools, ready to start tearing out walls. Too late then for second thoughts, but that didn't stop me from having them.

"Come on." Karen took my arm and gently pulled me toward the staircase in the storage area behind the shop. "You'll be back down in just a few minutes," she added as I pleaded work.

"Besides, Julie has everything under control."

Reluctantly, I followed her to the stairs and climbed up, like a condemned woman mounting the gallows.

CHAPTER 2

*I*t was far worse than I had imagined.

I surveyed the chaos that had once been my cozy apartment. The small balcony still looked out at the bay that gave Keyhole Bay its name; out there, boats rocked gently against their moorings in the afternoon sunlight, a momentary tourist lull giving the waterfront a sense of serenity and peace.

Inside the apartment? An entirely different matter. The place looked like the aftermath of a hurricane—something I had experience with here in the Florida panhandle.

Half of one interior wall was completely missing, the kitchen cabinets that had clung to it standing in the middle of my living room. The refrigerator was shoved up against the dining table, its power cord snaking through a jumble of small appliances crammed onto the remaining few feet of counter space to the single still-functioning outlet.

Next to the missing wall, the sink was still usable but its supporting counter rested on a makeshift framework where the cabinet had been removed.

It was amazing how much havoc three men could wreak in one day's work. Not even a full day; they'd started at eight but they'd knocked off early to go finish another job, promising to be back first thing tomorrow morning.

It wasn't as though Riley, Karen's former—and current—husband hadn't warned me. "Tim is a great renovations guy," he'd said when he gave me his friend's number. "But it's going to be a mess for a while. Do you remember when we did our bathroom?"

I didn't. Riley and Karen had remodeled the bathroom immediately after buying their house but before they moved in. I had seen both the before and after, but not the during.

"It got a lot worse before it got better," he'd warned me. "But you'll see," he'd patted my shoulder, "you'll be pleased with the results."

Now, standing in the ruins of my apartment, I wasn't so sure.

I watched Karen's face as she took in the disaster area, expecting the same shock and dismay I was feeling. Instead she gave me a lopsided grin. "Not too bad."

"What? It's a mess! I can't use the stove, the refrigerator is practically out on the balcony, and there isn't a bare inch of counter space anywhere."

"Riley warned you," she reminded me. "And this really isn't that bad. Your sink still works," she gestured at the makeshift arrangement, "and your fridge is functional. You can use the kitchen table for counter space. You'll manage for a few weeks."

"Weeks! Are you kidding me?" I knew I was whining, and I didn't care. One day in and I was already questioning my sanity.

"Relax." Karen put her arm around my shoulders. "When the demolition starts it's scary, but you'll get through it."

"But it's my turn to cook next week," I wailed. "How can I do that without a kitchen?"

"You'll use Jake's," she said matter-of-factly, referring to my boyfriend. "Won't be the first time, and won't be the last." She paused. "Unless he's moving in here full time after the remodel."

I shrugged. "We haven't really talked about it. I mean, I need more space with him staying here regularly, but we haven't discussed making it a permanent thing.

"We're still taking it slow."

Karen snorted and shook her head. "How long are you going to 'take it slow'?" Her fingers made air quotes around the phrase. "You've been a couple for how long? Two years? Three?"

I shrugged again.

When it came to romance, I was always a little slow. Make that a lot slow. In high school I'd been the third member of the couple that was Karen and Riley, and in the period that followed the death of my parents in senior year, I'd pretty much shut everyone out.

In the years since, I hadn't dated much. Until Jake. It was kind of hard to ignore the hunk who bought the bookstore across the street from Southern Treasures. He'd noticed me too, though it had taken us a while to become a couple.

Now Karen was talking about him moving into my place. I wasn't sure I was ready, but I couldn't say the idea hadn't occurred to me. Not that I was about to admit it.

"You're telling me what to do?" I laughed. "You and Riley wouldn't even admit you were back together for months and months."

Karen looked at me with a sheepish grin. "What can I say? For some people a marriage just doesn't 'take.' For us, it was the divorce that didn't last.

"But we had to be sure."

"And are you? Still sure, I mean?" I turned serious. I'd been Karen's maid of honor—for the second time—just a few months earlier.

"We are." She shook off the moment of solemnity and moved toward the hole where my kitchen wall used to be. "Now let's see what you've got planned over here."

I followed her as she made her way through the combat zone that used to be my kitchen. We stopped just the other side of the hole, looking across the gloomy expanse of exposed rafters above and loose plywood sheets below. "We're going to put the main living space over here," I said. "And the kitchen on the back of the wall where it is now, well where it was," I gestured to the hole in the wall. "We'll expand the balcony and put a half bath behind the new kitchen.

"The main space will be an open plan living/dining area with lots of room for friends and family.

"There's a staircase from the bakery kitchen for guest access, so we can make the other stairs a private entrance to the master suite."

"Master suite." Karen rolled her eyes. "Woo, fancy."

"Not really," I admitted. "Just turning the existing living room into a larger bedroom. Probably can't afford to do anything with the existing bathroom right now, or my bedroom, but we can make changes there later."

I led her back through the hole in the wall and down the stairs to Southern Treasures. "Don't you need to get to work?" I glanced at the cartoon-cat clock. "You still have the afternoon news to do."

"Get to work!" Bluebeard squawked from his cage. Apparently he was speaking to us again. "Get movin', girly."

Karen laughed and headed for the door. She glanced over her shoulder at Bluebeard. "Slave driver!" She opened the door and waved goodbye. "See you tonight."

Bluebeard mimicked her laugh as the door closed behind her. "Bye-bye, pretty girl," he called after her. Sometimes his social skills seemed extremely lacking.

"Bluebeard," I said warningly. At least he wasn't swearing. I should be grateful for small favors. Still, he knew better than to flirt with customers. He also knew Karen was practically family and he stretched the rules where family was concerned.

I suppose that made sense, since he really was family. Karen, and several other friends, knew Bluebeard was the spokesbird for the ghost of my great-uncle Louis Georges, the man who'd left me the majority share of the gift shop. And Bluebeard.

Julie, though, didn't know. She regularly brought her daughter Rose Ann into the shop and I wasn't sure how she'd feel about having the toddler around a ghost. It was getting harder to keep the secret from her and I knew it was only a matter of time before I would have to tell her.

But how? I fidgeted with the stock, straightening rows of glasses that were already perfectly aligned and checking T-shirts to make sure the sizes were in order, even though I knew Julie already had everything in order.

I inspected the postcard spinner and the case of vintage costume jewelry, and adjusted the price tags on a couple of the hand-made quilts hanging on the back wall.

It was my job as owner to check on my employees, right? I wasn't just avoiding talking to her, was I?

Of course I was. But what was I supposed to do, walk over and say, "Oh, by the way, there's a ghost here in the shop, and I haven't bothered to tell you for, um, the last three years"? Somehow that didn't seem like a good idea.

While I searched for a way to broach the subject, the bell over the front door rang again, granting me a reprieve.

"Saved by the bell," Bluebeard said. It still startled me when he sounded exactly like Uncle Louis, even after hearing it hundreds of time over the last few years. Not to mention how he seemed to know what I was thinking.

I shot the bird a sharp look before smoothing my face into a welcoming smile for our visitor. I quickly went from polite greeting to a big grin when I spied Jake walking toward me.

His long strides crossed the shop quickly, and he slipped an arm around my shoulders, bending down to plant a quick kiss on my lips.

"Hi, beautiful."

I felt a warmth creep up my neck and spread over my face. I was attractive enough, I suppose, but Jake had a way of making me feel that I really was beautiful.

Yeah, whatever I told Karen, I was a goner.

"Hi yourself..." I didn't get any further before Bluebeard's wolf-whistle interrupted my greeting.

"Bluebeard!" I turned back to confront him, but he'd retreated into his cage, his back to me.

"Trying to sleep," he muttered.

I shook my head. Bluebeard did pretty much as he pleased, and he knew he would get away with it as long as he was on his good behavior when there were customers in the shop. I still had to try, but deep down I knew I'd lost that battle long ago.

I turned back to Jake. "Playing hooky?" I asked.

"Quiet afternoon," he shrugged. "Janey's got everything under control. Thought you might have time for coffee, and maybe a tour of the construction site?"

"One day in and already everybody wants a tour." I glanced at Julie. She nodded. "Quiet here, too," she said. "I'll buzz if I need you."

I took Jake's hand. "You sure you want to see this mess?" I asked.

He grinned. "How bad can it be?"

I shook my head. He'd just have to see for himself.

I don't know quite what I was expecting, but it certainly wasn't a shrug, nod, and "Hmmm." Which was what I got.

Jake didn't seem at all concerned with the state of my destroyed apartment.

"It's horrible, isn't it?" I prodded.

"Not so much." Another shrug. "Believe me, I've seen lots worse."

"You've seen buildings completely destroyed by fires," I shot back. Jake had been a fire chief and an arson investigator before moving to Florida. Of course he'd seen worse. "That doesn't count."

"It counts," he said. "Besides, this is a fairly small project. It's not like you're moving plumbing or reinforcing a foundation. It's not much more than cosmetic."

"Cosmetic? You mean like putting lipstick on a pig?"

Jake laughed and kissed the top of my head. "Ever tried to put lipstick on a pig? This is lots easier."

"You're not the one who has to live with it," I said, pulling him through the hole in the wall. Even if he did move in, it wouldn't be until after the construction was finished. "And how would you even know that?

"Watch your step," I added as he walked across the loose plywood covering the beams in the unfinished area.

I gestured at the boxes piled against the far wall. "We found those up here when I bought the place from Miss Pansy, and I thought she'd take them, but she hasn't. I'm going to have to call Bradley and ask him what his mom wants me to do with them."

Jake eyed the haphazard pile warily. "Any idea what's in them?"

I shook my head. "They aren't mine and I have no business going through them. So no." I pointed to the stairs. "If you want coffee we better head downstairs. Some of us do have work to do."

We stepped cautiously across the plywood to the stairs. Jake followed me down to the kitchen, where the sweet scent of the morning's baking lingered in the air. Vanilla, cinnamon, faint notes of citrus, and spices I couldn't immediately identify seemed to be permanently imbedded in this place.

I loved the smell. As I inhaled, a wave of gratitude for Chloe, my manager, washed over me. She was happy to come in at dawn and bake the goodies that made Lighthouse Coffee popular with tourists and locals alike. She and Julie were my two godsends, and I knew how lucky I was to have them.

Jake and I waved a greeting to Chloe and grabbed a table by the window, looking out onto the sidewalk and Beach Books across the street. Light traffic flowed slowly past as tourists rubbernecked, taking in the row of quaint shops that made up Keyhole Bay's main drag.

A few minutes later, Chloe delivered a pair of vanilla lattes and two lemon scones.

"Nice to have someone who knows what 'the usual' is," Jake said as he laid some bills on the table.

"You really don't have to do that," I reminded him.

"You pay for books."

"That's different."

"How?"

I sputtered, trying for a coherent explanation, but there wasn't one today, and there hadn't been one in the dozens of times we'd already had this conversation. I was pretty sure there never would be one, but it wouldn't stop me from trying.

"Shall I pick you up for dinner?" Jake asked, finally letting me off the hook.

I shook my head. "Probably easier to take two cars."

Jake glanced toward the ceiling with the construction mess above. "You don't want to stay in that mess tonight, do you? Why don't I pick you up and bring you back to the shop in the morning?"

He had a point. I would have to get used to living in a combat zone, but I wasn't sure I was ready to face it the first night.

"I suppose that would work," I said, nodding. "But I'll have to be back early to let the contractor in. And I did promise to take Sly leftovers on my way home."

"He and Anna won't be at dinner?" Jake sounded disappointed. I didn't blame him. We were all fond of Sly, and when his old flame came back into his life last year we had all shared in his joy. The two of them were frequent guests at our regular Thursday dinners.

"He said they had some work to do at the cabin and weren't sure if they'd be back in time for dinner."

"We'll stop by on the way home then."

I finished my coffee and looked longingly at the untouched scone. "I don't want to completely spoil my dinner," I said. "Ernie's cooking is always a treat."

Jake bounced up and went to the counter, returning with a small white bag and a couple sheets of waxed paper. He expertly wrapped the scone, along with the remaining half of his own. "We'll have them for breakfast."

I smiled up at him and nodded. It was going to be a good evening.

Ninety minutes later I shooed Julie out the door. "Go relieve your mom," I told her. Anita Nelson loved her time with her granddaughter, even though the energetic toddler could be hard to keep up with. When Julie worked a full day, as she usually did on Thursdays, Anita was ready to hand Rose Ann back to her mom.

Julie chuckled. "She says she sleeps really good on the days Rose Ann is there."

"Pretty baby," Bluebeard chimed in. He was fond of the little girl, and she was one of his biggest fans.

"Not much of a baby anymore," Julie said, giving him a scritch on the top of his head. "Be good," she told him and headed for the door. "Have a good dinner," she called back as she left. "See you in the morning."

I locked up behind her, closed down the register, and put the cash drawer in the heavy antique safe under the stairs. Every year I had offers from customers asking to buy the safe, but it had been in the store since before Uncle Louis owned it, and I couldn't bear to part with it.

I spread a heavy blanket over Bluebeard's cage to block the glow from the streetlights that would filter in through the front window when it got dark, and settled him in for the night.

I offered him a few pieces of cut melon and a half-dozen grapes, a bribe for good behavior while I was out. He'd been known to make messes if I was gone longer than he thought necessary.

I cleaned and refilled his water dish, placing it inside the cage. He looked at the dish, then back at me. "Coffee?"

I shook my head. "You can't have coffee. It would make you very sick." I petted his head, feeling the silky feathers under my fingertips. "You know that."

He butted his head against my fingers. After a few silent moments, he let out a very human-sounding sigh. "I miss coffee."

My heart squeezed in my chest. "I know you do, Uncle Louis. But we can't get around this one."

He sighed again and took the last grape from his bowl, then retreated to his cage. He rattled around for a moment, getting comfortable, then glared at me, the moment gone. "Trying to $*$%^&$ sleep here," he grumped.

I raised my hands in mock surrender. "I'm leaving," I said. I checked the clock and grabbed my purse. Jake would be ready to go most any time.

CHAPTER 3

$\mathcal{I}$ set the alarms and locked the door behind me, stepping out onto the curb to wait for Jake, knowing I wouldn't return until early the next morning.

Bluebeard would complain that I stayed out all night, but I was used to that. It wasn't like I was a teenager breaking curfew, but occasionally he made me feel like it; or at least how I imagined it would feel. Having lost my parents while still in high school, I hardly had a normal frame of reference.

Jake pulled up a couple minutes later and I quickly climbed in. Jake took the first chance to pull off the highway that formed the main road and twisted his way through the narrow residential streets.

Every place in Keyhole Bay was five minutes from every other place in town, except during tourist season. Then it could stretch to twenty minutes or more. Locals learned to take the back streets or walk. Or schedule errands and appointments on weekday mornings. It wasn't unusual to spot friends in the grocery store on Wednesday, stocking up for the weekend.

"Have you heard from Sly?" Jake asked.

I shook my head. "He did say he'd call if they changed their plans, so I expect him back tonight."

I turned in my seat and looked at him. "Has he said anything to you about Anna?"

"Why would he say anything to me? I'm the new guy, remember?"

"Hardly new," I said. "You've been here a while. And you're the kind of person people talk to. Who did Riley come to for advice on planning his honeymoon?"

Jake shook his head. "Only because he wanted to know about California wine country and I used to live in the area."

"No, because he trusted you to keep a secret. Which you did." Jake hadn't even told *me* where Riley was taking Karen.

Jake made another turn and fell silent as he concentrated on threading his way along a street narrowed to a single lane by cars parked on both sides.

Two blocks later we pulled up outside Felipe and Ernie's house. Jake suggested I get out while he drove around the block looking for a parking place, but I waved away the suggestion. "Circle around and park in the alley," I said. "There's room there for a couple cars next to the back gate."

He followed my directions, and sure enough there was room to tuck his compact in next to Riley's pickup. Fortunately, Jake had a small car.

The top of the board-and-batten fence was over my head, but I knew where the pull-chain was for the latch. I reached over, tugged on the loop, and the gate swung inward on well-oiled hinges. From past experience, I knew opening the gate would set off a buzzer in the house.

At the kitchen window, Ernie spotted us and waved us inside. I slowed as we approached the house to admire the garden, wondering where they found time to keep up the flower beds and pots of herbs that lined the fences and patio.

We let ourselves into the screened-in patio and made our way through to the kitchen. Karen and Riley stood at one side of the spacious area, tall glasses of dark sangria in hand.

At the counter, Ernie shaped patties of ground meat. "Do not start with me," he said before I could even get my mouth open.

"It is summer, and it's hot, and there is no way I am firing up that monster," he waved one elegant hand at the massive commercial range that had been his Christmas gift a few months earlier, "no matter how beautiful she is."

I had to laugh. Ernie loved the range, loved that Felipe had bought it for him even though it overpowered the rest of the kitchen. But he was right about the heat. Summer had arrived in full force in the last couple weeks, and today had been a scorcher.

"So I assume we're getting burgers," I said, accepting a glass of sangria from Felipe. "I'm okay with that. Of course they aren't traditional Southern burgers, are they?"

I sipped the fruit-infused wine and nodded my approval. "Delicious. A glass or two of this and I'll be okay with whatever you cook."

"And just what is a traditional Southern burger?" Felipe asked as he passed a glass of sangria to Jake. "Is it topped with grits or okra? Besides," he continued, "I thought we agreed that we were going to broaden our horizons."

Jake tipped his glass toward me. "He does have a point. We were all having trouble putting together a menu that didn't duplicate anything we'd done before."

I held up my empty hand in surrender. "Okay. Okay. But may I just point out that I didn't start this line of conversation. He," I pointed at Ernie, "did. And I said I was okay with whatever he cooks."

I laughed again and added, "I'm always okay with whatever he cooks because it means I don't have to."

"Amen to that," Karen said.

I turned to her and saw a stricken look cross her face. "Not you cooking," she said hastily. "Me cooking."

She gave me a fake glare. "And you knew exactly what I meant, even if it wasn't what I said."

It was true. Karen had long claimed that her only domestic quality was that she lived in a house, and our dinner rotation was the one thing that forced her to regularly excavate the piles of paper, books, clothes, and general detritus that threatened to take over her house.

Although since she and Riley had remarried, it did seem that there was less panic each time her turn to host came around. Maybe Riley was being a good influence.

Or maybe he'd taken over some decluttering duties.

I turned back to Felipe and Ernie, who had their heads close together, talking quietly while I sparred with Karen.

"Anything we can do to help?" I asked.

They both jumped slightly, as though they'd forgotten we were there, and shook their heads.

"No," Felipe said. "Everything's under control. Ernie's got the burgers about ready, the grill is heating, salads are in the fridge with another pitcher of sangria," he ticked off on his fingers as he talked.

"Yep, under control."

"Well, you sure looked guilty about something," Karen said, her reporter's suspicions aroused.

"Care to share with the rest of the class?"

The two men exchanged a glance. Ernie shrugged, elegantly, as he did everything.

"It is up to you, cher."

Felipe fidgeted, clearly unsure.

"Okay, spill!" Karen commanded. Politicians and other ne'er-do-wells seldom held out under her grilling, and she knew Felipe and Ernie wanted to tell us whatever was on their minds.

They just needed the proper persuasion.

"We're waiting," she sing-songed, tapping her foot to underscore her impatience.

Felipe sighed.

"We wanted to wait for dessert," he said.

"Quit stalling," Karen shot back. "You know you want to tell us."

Ernie looked down at his partner and nodded. "We both knew we couldn't wait," he said. "You might as well tell them."

Felipe's customary confidence deserted him as everyone turned to him expectantly.

"You might as well get it over, buddy," Riley said. "She always ends up getting her way."

Karen gave her husband's shoulder a gentle punch.

"Really? I don't think so."

Riley wrapped one strong arm around her shoulders and hugged her. "You know you do."

Jake and I both nodded.

"He's right," Jake said to Felipe. "You're going to have to tell her or we'll never hear the end of this."

Felipe looked down at his shoes and back up at his partner.

He stood a little straighter and squared his shoulders. A faint, self-conscious smile touched his mouth and he drew a deep breath before he spoke again.

"Okay, if you just can't wait, I guess I have to tell you.

"We're getting married."

CHAPTER 4

"When?"
   "Where?"
"Congratulations!"
"How can we help?"

Dinner was forgotten as the kitchen erupted into chaos. We all tried to hug Felipe and Ernie at the same time, while everyone peppered them with questions, talking over each other.

"Hold on!" Ernie spoke over the din and held up a hand, palm out, as though to try and stem the tide of questions.

The din stopped for a moment, and he hurried ahead as though afraid it would erupt again. "We haven't made any plans yet," he said, smiling down at his partner. "But y'all will be the first to know, I promise."

He shook his head as Karen opened her mouth. "We really can't tell you what we don't know," he continued.

"Let's get these burgers on the grill," he picked up the tray of patties and headed toward the patio. "Then we'll tell you what we can."

A few minutes later, we were settled into the retro metal patio chairs on the screened porch. Ernie hovered near the door, keeping a wary eye on the grill, and Felipe made sure everyone's glasses were refilled before he sat down.

Karen cleared her throat impatiently and stared at them. "Well?"

Felipe reached for Ernie's hand before he answered. "It's not like we didn't want to get married," he said, his voice thick with emotion. "I love this man, we've been together for years, and it would seem like the logical next step.

"But we couldn't. Not here.

"At least until recently."

"We talked about going to another state," Ernie said. He continued talking as he stepped outside and flipped the burgers. "But that didn't seem right somehow. We didn't want to have to run away; we wanted to get married here, in our hometown, with all our friends around." He pointed to Karen and Riley. "Like you did."

"And now we can," Felipe said. "We don't know exactly when or where, but we do know that we want to share the day with our friends and family.

"And we consider all of you family."

Riley nodded in agreement. "I know how much that meant to us," he said, taking Karen's hand.

Silence descended, each of us lost momentarily in our own thoughts. I wondered if this was a conversation Jake and I would have to have someday and I wondered if I would ever be ready for it; and I wondered if anyone was ever *really* ready.

I quickly pushed the thought aside. I'd solved several mysteries in the past few years, but Jake—and our relationship—wasn't one of them.

Ernie broke the silence with a heartfelt curse from the other side of the screen wall.

We all jumped, and he looked over at us, one finger stuck in his mouth. "You know, this thing's hot!" he said, glaring at the grill over the stricken digit.

"News flash," Karen said drily.

Felipe had risen from his chair and was already through the door, but Ernie waved him off. "Startled me more than hurt," he said as he began loading a plate with the sizzling patties.

"Looks like it's time to eat." He handed the plate to Felipe and began loading another.

We trooped back to the dining room and helped our hosts ferry heaping bowls of salads and trays of burger toppings to the table.

As we took our places at the table, Riley stood beside his chair and raised his glass. "To the grooms."

We all raised our glasses and repeated, "To the grooms."

Conversation turned to the food, as it always did at the beginning of our meals. Ernie explained his process for the heavenly burgers—freshly ground beef, thick patties, lightly seasoned, and patience.

"When they're thicker, they take time to cook through. You turn 'em every couple minutes, maybe move them around if there are hot spots in the coals, but that's all you do. You don't fiddle with them, and you never, ever, squish them." He shuddered as though the very thought pained him.

We passed the chilled bowls of potato and macaroni salad, loaded our burgers with slices of tomato and sweet onion, and engaged in a friendly argument about whether ketchup did or did not belong on a burger.

Eventually the conversation circled back around to Felipe and Ernie's announcement.

"I wondered," Karen said, "when the court ruling came down. But you didn't say anything."

"We'd spent a lot of years not talking about it," Felipe explained. "We just accepted that it wasn't possible so it wasn't even a topic for discussion. Better not to wish for things we couldn't have."

"Then a few years ago things started changing," Ernie took over the story. "We even considered going up to Massachusetts, but like I said, we wanted our friends with us."

Felipe's voice held a tone of tamped-down anger as he continued. "And we didn't want to feel like we had to run away; like it was something shameful we were doing.

"So we stopped talking about it again, even though that denial was shameful in its own way."

"Until now," Ernie said softly. "Now we can do it right, we can do it proud." A happy grin lit up his face like the sun coming out from behind a cloud.

Felipe's answering smile seemed to wash away the anger and he nodded in agreement. "Now we can do it right."

"Glory's a pretty accomplished wedding planner now," Karen volunteered.

I shook my head. "Oh, no you don't, Freed. If anything, you're the one with wedding experience. Now that you've had two of them.

"Or maybe we could get your mother to help you."

At the mention of her mother, Karen's face fell. "You wouldn't dare," she said.

Her mother had flown in from Washington—the state, not D.C.—and nearly driven Karen crazy in the weeks before her wedding. Now, instead of being safely on the other side of the continent, her mother and Clint—also known as Stepdad Number Three—were transferring to Orlando. She would not only be on the same side of the continent, she would be in the same state.

"Oh, you won't be the wedding planners," Felipe assured us. "You two are going to be our maids of honor, if you will. And we all know Glory has some experience in that role!"

He had me there. Yes, I'd been Karen's maid of honor both times she married Riley. And though I didn't exactly love the experience, I was touched that he and Ernie wanted us to be part of their wedding.

"Of course," I said.

"Absolutely," Karen answered.

"And now," Ernie said, rising from his chair, "it's time for dessert."

He started a pot of coffee for Ernie, who always drank coffee with dessert, even in the middle of summer, and took a tray of square foil-wrapped packets from the counter.

He headed for the porch, calling back over his shoulder, "Three minutes on the grill. Be right back."

We took advantage of the interruption to clear the table and put away the leftover salads. With five of us working together, the dishes were stacked in the dishwasher and the bowls were in the refrigerator by the time Ernie returned.

He used a pair of grill tongs to place a foil bundle on each dessert plate, with the warning that they were very hot.

I carefully pulled at a corner of the foil, teasing up one side of the bundle. The aroma of melting chocolate and sweet vanilla tickled my nose, a familiar smell from somewhere long ago.

It took a few seconds as we each picked at the foil, trying to avoid burning our fingers, before Jake peeled back enough foil to identify the mystery dessert.

"S'mores?" he asked, looking at Ernie. "Are they s'mores?"

Jake didn't wait for an answer, but immediately scooped up the oozing graham cracker sandwich and took a bite.

Karen gave a squeal of delight and quickly bit into her hers—and instantly regretted her impulse. "Ohhh, hmphff," she said, fanning her hand in front of her mouth. "Vrrgh huhhmpt."

"Hot?" I asked helpfully.

She gave me a dirty look and kept fanning as she dropped the graham cracker and grabbed her sangria, washing down the hot marshmallow with a gulp of chilled wine.

She drew a deep breath, but before she could speak, her cell phone rang from the depths of her purse in the living room. With her closest friends at the table, the chances were good it was the station. She jumped up without a word and sprinted for the phone.

The rest of us continued with dessert, approaching the hot s'mores with a bit more caution.

A minute later Karen hollered from the living room. "Gotta go. Riley?"

"He can ride back with us," Jake answered.

"Thanks!"

The back door slammed behind her and seconds later we heard Riley's truck roar to life in the alley.

Riley laughed nervously. "I hope nobody's parked too close."

"I'm next to you," Jake said. "But there's room to get around me."

Riley winced. "I hope so."

We all waited a moment, but when there was no crash from the alley, we went back to our dessert.

The marshmallow was no longer volcanic, and we spent several laughter-filled minutes dealing with the sticky, gooey sandwiches and sharing stories of eating s'mores when we were kids. It seemed they were a universal experience, no matter where we grew up.

The conversation moved on to the latest tourist antics. Most of the visitors to Keyhole Bay were great. They came to enjoy the beautiful weather, spent their vacation money in the shops and motels and restaurants, and generally kept the local economy alive.

But there were always a few that provided head-shaking stories. "I had someone come down to the dock the other day," Riley told us. "Came right up to the gangplank and wanted to know if he could charter *Ocean Breeze* for a party.

"I told him there were plenty of party boat charters, that this was a fishing vessel. He said he'd already looked at those, but they wanted too much money. Thought since my boat wasn't as new and shiny I should be a lot cheaper."

He shook his head. "I didn't have the heart to tell him how wrong he was."

"I know what you mean," Felipe said, nodding. "I am constantly amazed by the people who think because we are in a small town, Ernie and I don't know the value of what's in our shop. Like somehow we just landed here and shoved a bunch of old junk in the door and put inflated price tags on it."

He paused for a minute, then went on. "Not that there aren't people in town who haven't done just that. But they usually don't last long."

He didn't have to name names. We all knew the gory details of a small antique shop that had opened a few blocks over from Carousel Antiques, the upscale shop Felipe and Ernie had run for more than a decade. The "Coming Soon" banner draped across the storefront lasted longer than the store did, and the owners disappeared back to

Miami, leaving a trail of unpaid bills, angry suppliers, and a few disgruntled customers.

Throughout our conversation, Riley kept checking his phone every few minutes, as though somehow staring at the screen would make Karen call or text.

Jake noticed his preoccupation and caught my eye. I immediately understood his look.

I got up and took some plastic containers from Ernie's carefully-arranged cupboard. "I promised Sly I'd bring leftovers," I reminded him, hauling salad bowls from the refrigerator. "He wasn't sure he'd be back from the cabin in time for dinner, but he said he 'purely regretted' missing your cooking."

Ernie grinned and jumped up to help me. We quickly packed up containers of salad, some burger patties wrapped in foil, and a couple of the s'mores still vaguely warm from the grill.

Ernie took a cloth bag from a neat stack in another cupboard, placing a Mason jar of sangria in the bottom and packing the food in carefully. "Tell Sly he can just send this back when it's convenient."

It took several more minutes for us to say our goodbyes. As we were leaving, Felipe reminded me it was my turn to cook next week. I must have looked as stricken as I felt, because he instantly put an arm around my shoulders. "Are you okay, chica?"

"It's just, if you could see the mess that used to be my kitchen—"

"We'll cook at my place this time," Jake cut in, his arm around my shoulders. "They started the demolition this morning," he reminded the others, "and the place is a bit disrupted."

"Disrupted?" I snorted. "The entire place is a disaster area, and I am already questioning my sanity in doing this."

Riley gave my shoulder a squeeze. "It looks terrible for a while, then it starts to come together, I promise."

I wanted to believe him, but my brain kept giving me images of the destruction I'd seen earlier in the day. "I'll take your word for it," I said. But I don't think I really meant it.

Riley snuck another look at his phone, trying to hide his impatience, but we all knew better.

"We better get going," I said. "Do you want us to drop you off before we go to Sly's?"

Riley hesitated for just a moment and I had my answer.

I reached for Sly's bag, but Riley beat me to it. "Least I can do," he said sheepishly.

CHAPTER 5

The ride to Riley's was short, but the tension in the car was palpable. The conflict between their jobs had contributed to Riley and Karen's breakup before; it was clear Riley was struggling with the adjustment and determined not to let it happen again.

Karen's SUV was in the driveway, but no sign of the truck. At least Riley wasn't stranded.

"Tell her to text me when she gets home," I said as Riley climbed out of the back seat. "I worry about her too."

He laughed, a bit harshly, and nodded. "Will do."

As we pulled away, Jake patted my knee. "That was good of you to say. He needs to know he isn't the only one."

"Well, I do worry about her. She forgets everything, including her own safety, when she's on a story. Around here that usually isn't anything more dangerous than a contentious city council meeting, but lately..." my voice trailed off as I thought about the dicey situations Karen and I had gotten ourselves into.

Granted, it was usually me that ended up in the hospital or talking to police chief Barclay "Boomer" Hardy. But Karen had had her share of close calls, and she was fearless when she was chasing down a story.

It only took a couple minutes to get back out on the highway that formed the main street of Keyhole Bay. Late in the evening on a week-night, even in June, traffic was light.

We were still a few blocks from Sly's junkyard behind Fowler Auto Sales when we spotted the emergency lights.

"Looks like another tourist had a run in with Keyhole Bay's finest," I said.

"Yeah, and they pulled him over right in front of Fowler's," Jake said. "Hope they're not blocking the gate."

But as we got closer, it quickly became apparent that there was more than one set of lights. This was more than a routine traffic stop, and they were in Fowler's lot, not on the street in front.

Half a block from the driveway, a uniformed deputy directed traf-fic. Behind him, nosed into the curb, I spotted Riley's truck.

Whatever was going on here had warranted a callout from the station for Karen. That meant trouble.

Beyond the deputy, I could see several vehicles massed in the parking lot: sheriff's vehicles, a paramedic unit, and an ambulance. The strobing lights played over groups of uniformed law enforcement and medical personnel, but I couldn't spot Karen in the chaos.

And it was all way too close to my friend Sly's home.

Jake pulled up next to the deputy and stopped, opening his window at a gestured request from the officer.

"Road's closed," he said. "Do you need directions to go around?"

"No sir," Jake answered. "I know the way."

I leaned across the seat, fear rising in my throat. Fowler's should have been closed hours ago, the employees gone for the day. That only left Sly and his dog Bobo.

"What happened?" I asked, unable to control the tremor in my words.

"Don't rightly know. They just assigned me to direct traffic. Not that's there a lot to do," he said, glancing around at the empty streets. "Gonna have to ask you to move along now."

Jake looked at me and I shook my head. "It's got to be Sly," I said. "I can't leave until I know what's going on."

Jake nodded at me and turned back to the deputy. "Thanks."

He put the car in reverse, backed up a few feet, and made a highly illegal U-turn. The deputy watched him closely, but made no move to object to the maneuver.

Jake drove a block and turned left onto a side street that paralleled the side of the used car lot. A tall hedge shielded the lot and the junkyard beyond it from view.

Jake pulled up against the curb and killed the engine. "I don't suppose there's any way to talk you out of this."

I shook my head in the darkened car. It didn't matter whether or not he could see me; he knew what the answer would be.

Sly was my one connection to Uncle Louis—well, my *other* connection if you counted the ghost that lived in Southern Treasures —and he had become a big part of the family I'd created for myself after my parents died.

I had to go.

Jake sighed in resignation and climbed out of the car. "At least you're not going alone," he said. He pulled a beat-up flashlight from the glove compartment. "I don't know how good the batteries are," he said. "But it's better than nothing."

We locked the car, glanced around the still-empty street, and crossed over to the hedge.

My heart sank as I realized how thick it was. Emergency lights strobed through the dense branches, dimly illuminating the dense tangle in front of us.

Even the light couldn't find a way through. What hope did two full-size humans have?

CHAPTER 6

We walked back and forth along the hedge, looking for a break that would let us slip through, without success. Beyond the other side of the barrier, we could hear the voices of deputies and emergency crews calling to each other as they went about their duties.

"Maybe I should text Karen," I suggested. Somehow I felt the need to whisper, even though we were clearly alone and the noise in the lot would cover our conversation.

"She isn't answering Riley," Jake reminded me. "What makes you think she'll answer you?"

"She might," I answered.

"Especially if I tell her I'm here and I want to know if Sly is okay."

I didn't need to see Jake's expression to know his reaction, and I didn't need him to tell me it was a weak argument. Karen was focused on her story and nothing short of a much bigger story was going to get her attention.

I shrugged and went back to searching for a break in the hedge. I moved farther from the highway, away from the lights and noise in the lot.

I tried to remember exactly what was on the other side, but I hadn't really explored Sly's yard. If I was guessing correctly, we were just a few feet from the high chain-link fence that surrounded the yard, but I couldn't be sure.

Farther along the street, I found a low passage where the lower branches of the hedge were broken away. "Jake," I called in a hoarse whisper, "I think I found something. Is that flashlight working?"

He slid the switch and the flashlight cast a sickly yellow beam a few feet into the void. I couldn't see the other side, but there appeared to be a space large enough for me to wiggle through.

"I'm going to try it," I said.

"Not sure I can fit through there," Jake said, eyeing the opening. "You sure about this?"

"Not really," I admitted, dropping to my knees. "But I can't exactly stroll past the cops, can I?"

"That might be easier."

Unfortunately, Jake was right. Not only couldn't he get through there, I couldn't either. I shoved my shoulders into the gap and wiggled forward, but I quickly realized there was no way I could make it through.

I pushed myself back out, broken branches grabbing at my shirt and nearly stripping it off before I finally got clear.

"For a minute I thought I was going to have to pull you out of there," Jake said, helping me to my feet.

"Now can I text Karen?"

Jake shook his head, the movement a vague shadow in the darkness. "Not that it will do any good," he said. "But go right ahead."

I hate it when he's right.

Tears of frustration stung the back of my eyelids, and worry for Sly blocked out every other consideration. If sneaking past the cops was my only choice, then that was what I would have to do.

"Let's go," I said.

We walked back toward the highway. As we neared the end of the hedge where the lights could finally reach us, Jake clamped his hand on my shoulder to stop me.

Before I could question what he was doing, he started picking something out of my hair. "You don't want to answer questions about these if they see you," he explained, showing me a handful of twigs and dry leaves.

"Thanks."

I slipped around the end of the hedge and stood still, taking in the scene in front of me.

Activity seemed to be centered on the back of Fowler's building, away from the gate to Sly's junkyard. Maybe it wasn't as bad as I had feared. Maybe Sly and Bobo were okay.

But if they were okay, what was going on in the closed auto dealership?

And what was so important that Karen wasn't answering her phone?

I slipped my phone out of my pocket and called the one person who, until right this moment, I'd been afraid to call.

Sly.

He answered on the first ring. "I been expecting you to call, girl."

"Are you okay?" I asked, my voice shaky. "There are all these police cars and ambulances out here..." My voice trailed off as I tried to control myself.

"I'm just fine," he said. "Wishing I had me some of Mr. Ernie's cookin', but that's about the worst of it.

"You tell that sheriff that I'm expecting you, and he better let you come on back. Okay?"

I chuckled in spite of myself. Leave it to Sly to get directly to what was important.

Ernie's cooking.

I sent Jake to get the bag of leftovers from the car while I waited on the edge of the lot. So far no one had challenged us, but I didn't want to draw attention to us until I absolutely had to.

The minute Jake left my side I began to shake. I'd managed to hold the fear at bay while I was *doing* something. But the minute I stopped doing and relaxed, the awful realization of what might have been weakened my knees and sent shivers through me in spite of the temperature.

I waited in the shadows for Jake to return as my trembling lessened and some semblance of calm returned. Whatever was wrong, my friends were safe. I tried to hold on to that thought.

The touch of a hand on my arm sent my heart racing again. I whirled around, ready to defend myself.

"Whoa! Easy there!"

Jake.

I'd been so lost in my own thoughts I hadn't heard him approach. I guess I wasn't that calm after all.

He held up the bag with Sly's leftovers. "Ready when you are, slugger," he teased.

We moved along the hedge, staying as far away from the commotion as possible. We were nearly to Sly's gate when one of the deputies glanced our direction. He did a double take, as though he didn't believe someone would slink along the edge of their investigation, and trotted toward us.

"Act like you don't see him," I hissed at Jake, dragging him by the hand toward the gate. "Maybe we can get through the gate before he catches us."

"Not likely," Jake muttered back. "Unless we run, which would definitely look suspicious."

Did I mention how much I hate it when he's right?

The deputy caught up with us a few yards from the fence, planting himself directly in our path. I knew most of Boomer's deputies, but I didn't recognize this one.

We were close enough it felt like I could almost reach out and touch the gate, but we couldn't get past the solid wall of khaki uniform in front of us.

"What are you doing here?" he demanded. Without waiting for a reply, he bulled ahead. "You have to leave. Right now!"

"We're visiting a friend," Jake said evenly, gesturing with the bag in his hand. "Just bringing him some supper."

"Mighty late for supper," the deputy answered, his hand straying to the holster on his hip. "Why are you really here?"

"Just stopping to see our friend," Jake repeated. His voice was low and calm, but I could see his knuckles whiten as he gripped the bag tighter.

"He's expecting us," I said. "How about I call him and ask him to come out?" I held up the phone in my hand.

Wrong move.

I instantly found myself staring at the business end of a pistol that from my perspective looked about the size of a tank.

I froze.

Time stretched like warm taffy as I stared at the pistol.

"It's just a phone," I managed to choke out.

Beside me I could feel the tension coming off Jake, but he didn't move a muscle.

"Martine, what in the pluperfect hell are you doing here?" Boomer called across the parking lot.

In my peripheral vision I sensed movement but I was afraid to look away from the deputy, afraid to break eye contact with the twitchy man long enough to look toward the gruff voice.

"Simonds!" The voice was much closer now, the tone urgent and commanding. "Stand down! At once!"

We held our positions for a few seconds longer as Boomer hurried into view, then the deputy slowly lowered his weapon. His hand trembled as he carefully reholstered the pistol and snapped the flap shut.

"My apologies, ma'am," he said. "But you are intruding on an active investigation, and I must ask you to leave."

Boomer stepped between us, his presence edging Deputy Simonds —at least he had a name now—back a couple steps. Boomer turned and shot a quick look at the deputy. I couldn't see Boomer's face, but Simonds's expression was clear: he knew he'd be explaining himself to Boomer sometime in the very near future, and he wasn't looking forward to the conversation.

Boomer whipped back to stare at me. "You haven't answered my question, girl. What are you two doing here?"

I'd had run-ins with Boomer before, several involving homicide investigations. He wasn't given to preamble or subtlety but he had an ironclad sense of honor and a definite soft spot for the residents of "his" town. Still, it appeared we had stumbled into one of his investigations and he never took kindly to what he saw as meddling.

"Sorry, Sheriff Hardy," Jake answered before I could calm myself enough to speak. "We promised Sly we'd bring him leftovers from supper," he waved the bag once more. "We didn't even know there was anything going on until we got here."

My silent prayers were belatedly answered at that moment when the subject of our conversation himself appeared at the gate in front of us.

"Hardy, are you keeping my guests out of my yard?" Sly called out from behind the unlocked gate.

A grin turned up the corners of Boomer's mouth for a split second, quickly suppressed as he turned to face Sly.

"Not tryin' to be impertinent, you understand, but I am purely about to pass out from hunger, and that boy there has my supper," Sly gestured at Jake.

We all knew Sly was exaggerating, and he made no effort to hide the grin that split his dark face, exposing gaps where he'd lost a couple teeth.

"Hey, old man," Boomer shot back. "These two just keep getting in the way of my investigations. I gotta keep an eye on them so's they don't mess up this one."

I swallowed hard and risked speaking. "What happened, anyway?"

"Don't know yet," Boomer replied, though it was obvious he knew something he wasn't telling us.

I didn't press him. At this point all I wanted was to get safely into Sly's house and away from the twitchy Deputy Simonds.

"We won't keep you any longer," Boomer said, clearly dismissing us. "You go on back to Mr. Sly's now, and we'll get back to our work."

He didn't have to ask me twice. I grabbed Jake's hand and we hustled through the gate into the junkyard. Boomer watched us until we were through the gate, then gestured Simonds to follow him and walked back toward the flashing lights.

CHAPTER 7

$\mathcal{N}$one of us spoke until we were safely inside Sly's home with the door closed and locked.

I was always startled by the contrast between the plain cinder-block exterior of the house and the cozy interior full of rattan, bright colors, and lush houseplants. It was a far cry from the eccentric-bachelor decor I had expected on my first visit.

Sly took the bag of leftovers from Jake and stashed them in the refrigerator in his spotless kitchen.

"I thought you were hungry," I said.

"I might be," Sly replied, carrying a tray of homemade lemonade back into the living room. "But I can wait a spell while I find out what all the commotion is about."

"We hoped you knew," Jake said. He helped himself to a glass of lemonade. "Thanks."

Sly shook his head and lowered himself into his favorite chair. Bobo padded over and rested his massive head on Sly's lap in a bid for pets.

"Don't know nothin'," Sly said, petting the big dog's head. "Got home about an hour ago, everything was quiet. Next thing I know, there's lights and sirens over at Fowler's. I went out to take a look, but all I could see from here was a bunch of uniforms running around and shouting at each other.

"Didn't much want to get in the middle of it so I came back inside to wait for you. 'Bout then you called and I went out to meet you." He shrugged and took a long pull on his lemonade. "That's all I know."

"We don't know much more than that." Jake went on to describe our attempts to get into the yard, ending with, "And that's when you came out and yelled at Sheriff Hardy."

"I didn't yell at him," Sly protested. "I just spoke up so that old boy could hear me over the racket his crew was making."

He turned his attention to me. "You tried to crawl through the hedge?"

I smiled to cover my embarrassment, but I could feel a blush tinge my face pink. "Yeah," I admitted in a sheepish tone. "I was getting worried about you and Bobo, what with all the emergency vehicles."

"Sooo," Jake drew the word out as he looked from me to Sly. "None of us know what's going on out there. The cops and rescue units have been out there for almost an hour without an ambulance leaving, which means they aren't in any hurry. And they won't let anyone near the place.

"Not good."

"And Karen got a call that sent her running out without an explanation," I reminded him. "If I was a betting woman, I'd put money on her snooping around over there."

"Which would explain why she's not answering her phone," Jake said, nodding his head. "Though that won't make Riley feel any better."

"Nope."

I stopped to explain the situation to Sly. "We took him home, but I think this is the first time he's had to deal with a call like that since they got married again. He's kind of having a hard time of it."

"It can be hard to adjust to," Jake said. "Being with someone who can run away at any moment."

I wondered if he was talking about Karen, or about himself. Jake was part of the Keyhole Bay volunteer fire department, and I'd already experienced a few of those calls.

I turned to Sly, determined to change the subject. "How's Anna? You were missed at dinner."

"She's fine," he said, with a grin that lit up his whole face. "Just fine.

"Sorry we missed dinner—"

My phone rang, stopping him in midsentence. I grabbed it from my pocket and glanced at the screen as I punched the answer button.

"Karen," I said, letting the two men know who was calling. "Where are you?"

"Almost to the house," she answered. "Boomer told me you were here, so I headed back as soon as I was finished. I have to get to the station and do a breaking news segment, but I wanted to let you know what's going on."

I was halfway to the door when she knocked a few seconds later. I opened the deadbolt and let her in, locking it behind her. Better safe than sorry.

Although her expression was somber, the rush of a big story had clearly energized her.

She didn't waste time on niceties, but immediately blurted out her news.

"Matt Fowler is dead."

CHAPTER 8

*D*ead? That didn't seem possible. Matt Fowler was only a few years older than me.

"What happened?" I'm not sure which one of us said it first, but we all asked.

Karen shook her head. "Nobody's saying. But it sure looks like *something* did. They wouldn't let me near the building, and there's a small army of paramedics and police over there."

"So what do you know?" I asked.

"Darn little," she admitted. "He was found in the service area by 'a family member,'" she used her fingers to put air quotes around the phrase, "and they called authorities.

"Beyond that, Boomer just kept saying 'No comment.'"

"And that rates pulling you away from dinner and a breaking news segment?" My dislike for the late Mr. Fowler was evident in my tone.

"Memaw always said not to speak ill of the dead," I went on, "but she also said if I couldn't say something nice, I shouldn't say anything at all. So I better shut up."

"Whatever else he is—was," Jake corrected himself, "Fowler Auto Sales is a big deal in this town. Anything that concerns Matthew Fowler concerns Keyhole Bay."

"Boy knows what he's talking about," Sly agreed. "Whatever happened to Mr. Fowler is big news."

"Which is why I have to get to the station."

I unlocked the door and she dashed out, her mind already on the newscast ahead. She didn't even bother to say goodbye.

After she was gone we tried to resume our conversation, but we were all focused on the bomb Karen had dropped in the middle of our evening. We kept circling back to the subject of Matthew Fowler, despite our complete lack of any facts.

"Was he sick?" Jake asked. Both Sly and I shook our heads.

"Not that I know of," I said.

"Saw him first of the week," Sly said. "Seemed to be fine. But people keep their ailments to themselves most of the time. Not that it stops the gossip from going around. But I ain't heard anything."

"It could have been some kind of accident, I suppose." I shrugged. "I remember how mad he got when Ernie and I were out in the service area, yelling at Ernie about how many ways we could get hurt, though I think he was more worried about his own finances than our health.

"Still, that shop could be a dangerous place."

Sly nodded his agreement.

"Wonder what he was doing there at this hour on a Thursday?" Jake said. "In his office, maybe, but out in the service area?"

I shrugged. "No way for us to know. Wish Karen could have given us a little more—" I stopped short. "Did she call Riley, I wonder."

I grabbed my phone and checked the messages. Nothing from Karen—she'd made that flying visit instead—and nothing from Riley.

Better safe than sorry, I thought, pulling up Riley's number.

He answered on the first ring.

"She called me," he said, knowing what I was going to ask. "Told me about Fowler and said she had to go to the station but she'd be home soon.

""That was your question, wasn't it?" There was a hint of self-aware amusement in his voice. "It may take some time, but I will get used to this, Glory."

Relieved, I let him know that I'd talked to Karen. "Did she tell you anything more than what she told us?" I asked. "All she said was that Fowler was dead and he'd been found by a family member in the service area."

"That's all I know, too."

We said our goodbyes, and soon after Jake and I said goodnight to Sly and Bobo and headed for the car.

This time no deputy tried to stop us as we made our way back along the edge of the property and around the corner to Jake's car, staying as far as possible from the cluster of uniformed men and official vehicles.

A few minutes later we pulled into the carport of Jake's rented bungalow and went inside.

Late as it was, neither of us was quite ready to turn in. The events of the evening had left us both with jangled nerves and an adrenaline hangover.

We finally went to bed about an hour later, assuring each other that things would surely look better in the morning.

Famous last words.

CHAPTER 9

*N*othing looked better on Friday, morning or evening. The story of Fowler's death made the front page of the *Keyhole News and Times*, and it led every news broadcast. It even hit the evening news out of Pensacola, though I suspected it must have been a slow news day in the big city.

Still, there were no details, no cause of death, nothing to answer the question of what happened.

I saw Karen late Saturday afternoon, but Boomer still hadn't released any information and she wasn't happy.

"People want to know," she grumbled as she helped me shut down after a busy day. "Seems like it's the only thing anyone wants to talk about."

I locked the door and cast an eye along the shelves. There were gaps that needed filling, but they could wait until morning. I'd missed lunch because of the crowds in the store, Tim the contractor had rendered my kitchen completely unusable, and I desperately wanted to sit down somewhere quiet and eat.

"I promise I won't ask," I said. "Let me get Bluebeard settled in and we can get out of here."

"No rush," she said. "Riley called a few minutes ago and said Neil's

Pizza is backed up. He probably won't make it home for at least another half hour."

"Is that with or without traffic?" I asked.

"Don't know. Either way, we have some time."

"I should let Jake know."

I refilled Bluebeard's water dish, grabbed a bowl of cut-up melon from the refrigerator in the storage area, and went in search of my phone.

"Riley already called him," she said. "They'll meet us at our house.

"I assume you're staying at Jake's again tonight?"

"Probably." I tried to sound casual. Truth be told, I was enjoying how comfortable it felt to go home with Jake every night. But it meant leaving Bluebeard alone, which could be dangerous if he decided to act up because I was gone.

I went through my usual end-of-day ritual with Bluebeard, giving him pets and treats and covering his cage against the streetlights.

He made his usual plea for coffee and I told him no. We had had that conversation so often I wondered if he even cared any more, or if it was just habit.

"I'm going to have to start staying home, though. Can't expect Jake to put me up forever.

"But unless I want to start washing dishes in the bathtub I won't be doing much cooking."

"How is the work coming upstairs?" Karen asked.

"It's awful. They moved the kitchen sink yesterday—but it isn't connected, hence the idea of washing dishes in the bathtub—and pulled the cabinets off the wall.

"That's one of the reasons I need to start staying here. We're going to reuse those cabinets instead of buying new ones, and if I refinish them myself, I can save a little money. But I have to be home to do that."

Karen laughed. "Do you have any idea *how* to do that?"

"I'll learn," I said.

My answer brought more laughter. "That I'd like to see."

I set the alarm and turned on the night-lights.

"Time to go." I grabbed my purse and stuck my phone in my pocket. "You ready?"

I was nearly to the door when Bluebeard spoke up. "Watch out, there's woman trouble."

Karen and I looked at each other and I walked back over to his cage.

"What did you say?"

"Woman trouble. Some people, it's always woman trouble." For once he repeated himself when I asked, though it didn't make any more sense the second time.

"What the heck does that mean?"

But as always Bluebeard—or Uncle Louis—refused to elaborate on his cryptic warning.

I tried again. "Tell me what you mean? What people? What kind of woman trouble?"

Bluebeard retreated into the dark recess of his cage and tucked his head under his wing, a signal that he was through talking and wanted to be left alone.

"Bluebeard?"

There was a short burst of profanity from deep inside the cage. "Trying to #&&^%%$# sleep here!"

CHAPTER 10

We beat both Jake and Riley to the house, though only by a couple minutes. I had just pulled the wine glasses from the cupboard and Karen hadn't even got the bottle open when the two men came through the front door together.

Like everyone else in town, they were talking about the death of Matthew Fowler.

Riley put the pizza box on the counter and greeted his wife with a kiss. Before I could warn him, he asked, "Have you heard anything more about Fowler?"

I expected an explosion, but Karen surprised me, and maybe herself.

"Nothing new," she said with a shake of her head. "The station manager is on me for more, but I can't broadcast what I don't know, and if Boomer knows anything, he isn't sharing."

"How about you?" I turned to Jake. "You're on the fire department. Have you heard anything from the guys that were out there Thursday night?"

Jake hesitated, looking uncomfortable.

"You did hear something! Come on, tell us."

He didn't say anything for a long minute, and I thought he was going to refuse. He would have been right to do so; it wasn't his place to release information the sheriff was keeping confidential. Still, we all wanted to know what he'd heard.

"I swear to you," Karen said, "I will not breathe a word until the sheriff makes his announcement. Or until I have another source."

Jake poured himself a glass of wine, clearly stalling. He sipped, set the glass down, and let out a long sigh.

"I don't know anything, not officially," he said. "I haven't talked to anyone directly, and it's nothing more than overheard gossip."

"But?" Riley urged.

"A couple of the guys were in the store this afternoon, and they were talking. Not to me exactly, but since there wasn't anyone else in the place they didn't bother to keep their voices down.

"I think they were both on the crew that night, and it sounds like it was ugly." He paused, as though remembering their words. "Nasty ugly. The kind that stays with you for a long while."

I could hear the voice of experience in his words. His years as a firefighter, paramedic, and arson investigator had provided more than enough unshakable memories, the kind he didn't share with anyone.

He shook his head. "No, I can't talk about this before dinner. Not if any of you want to be able to eat. But I promise I'll tell you what I know. Later."

"I doubt you're going to upset me," Riley said with a laugh. "Remember, I spend my days ankle deep in fish and I eat in the galley of a fishing boat. Not much bothers me."

"And I've seen crime scenes and accident scenes," Karen reminded him. "But it sounds like this isn't a conversation to have while we're eating."

"I agree. Dinner first," I said. My stomach growled in agreement.

We gathered around Karen's prized dinette set. The red Formica top and chrome edging testified to the fact that the set was older than we were, but it carried its age well. The chairs had been reupholstered a few years earlier, replacing the cracked and fading plastic with a modern equivalent, but they still creaked satisfactorily when you moved in your seat.

We kept the conversation light. When Riley mentioned the remodel, I did my best to convey the hopeless mess that was my formerly-tidy home, but he laughed it off.

"In a few weeks you won't even remember it," he said. "You'll just be so happy with the new space."

I wasn't convinced.

We reduced the pizza to a single forlorn piece in a matter of minutes—clearly I hadn't been the only one who was hungry—and emptied the bottle of wine. Karen replaced the empty bottle with a full one, set a tray of sliced melon on the table for dessert, and sat back down.

"OK, Jake. Time to spill."

The mood turned somber, and a shadow passed over Jake's features, clouding his blue eyes. But Jake was a man of his word and he began, choosing his words carefully.

"Like I said, a couple of the guys came in the store this afternoon. I'm sure they figured it was okay to talk in front of me, since I'm part of the department."

"You're more than that, Jake. You're an experienced professional in a bunch of volunteers. You're more of a chief than anyone in that department, including the chief. And he's told me that himself, several times," Karen said. "They probably figured you already knew."

Jake shrugged off the explanation. "Maybe so.

"Anyway," he continued, "they were talking about the scene at Fowler's.

"Someone, they thought it was the son, had gone looking for him when he wasn't answering his phone. They went to the dealership and found him in one of the service bays.

"You know the layout there, don't you?"

We all said we did.

"You know those lifts? The ones they use to raise cars so they can work underneath? There are three or four of them in the service bays—"

"Four," I interrupted him. "I got a good look at them a few years ago. When Jimmy Parmenter worked there."

He nodded at me. The memory didn't make either of us very happy. Jimmy was now serving a life sentence at Raiford for murder, and I'd helped put him there, but not before he tried to kill me too.

"Well, Fowler was under one of the lifts. Looked like he'd been working on a car and the whole thing came down on him."

A low curse escaped Riley's lips. "You're right. Ugly."

"How could that happen?" Karen asked.

I looked over at her and could see the reporter mask settle into place. She had a way of distancing herself from the unpleasant things she covered in her work life, and she used that skill as a buffer from the horror of how Fowler had died.

"Don't those things have to have interlocks and safety measures?" she continued. "Aren't they inspected? It seems like they'd be regulated and monitored all the time."

"I don't know what the rules are here in Florida," Jake said. "But I think they come under both state and federal safety regulations. That was one of the things the guys were talking about—which agency was going to take over the investigation. They didn't think the state or the Feds would let Boomer run the show."

I groaned. I'd already seen firsthand what happened when Boomer butted heads with an outside agency. And Jake was talking about state *and* federal groups.

The fight over jurisdiction could be a battle royale.

"That will not be pretty," I said.

Riley frowned. "Remember when the Feds tried to grab Bobby?" Two years ago, Riley's brother had been the prime suspect in the murder of an undercover federal agent and Boomer hadn't taken what he saw as their interference well. "This is gonna be worse."

"But if it's a safety violation, that isn't even in Boomer's jurisdiction. He might not like it, but it isn't like they're actually cutting him out of the investigation," I said. "Not that it will matter to Boomer."

"He's just protective of his town," Jake said in Boomer's defense. "Remember, he's the one that kept the Feds from grabbing Bobby and taking him out of town."

"Yeah," Riley agreed. "I was pretty pissed at him when he arrested

Bobby, but afterward it seemed like he was just trying to keep him here in town and not in some federal lockdown until they caught the right guys."

The conversation shifted from the details of Fowler's death to the mechanics of the accident. It was as though none of us wanted to think too much about the scene in the service bay.

Jake was right. It was ugly, and we all had pictures in our heads that would stick with us for a long time.

CHAPTER 11

*J*ake invited me to his place, but I didn't want to leave Bluebeard alone another night. I was already pushing my luck being gone two nights in a row, and there was no telling what kind of retaliation I would face if I didn't come home.

Besides, I told him, I couldn't just move into his place until my remodel was complete.

"Why not?"

A simple question, but it implied so much more.

"For one thing, I have a business to run."

"I run a business right across the street. And I commute every day. So that can't be the answer." He kept his eyes on the road, as though this was just a casual conversation.

"And then there's Bluebeard. He doesn't like it when I stay out overnight. Imagine how he'd behave if I was gone every night for a couple weeks."

"More likely a couple months," Jake said. "But no matter how long, he'll get over it. He'll adjust. Besides, Uncle Louis likes me."

"I don't think he completely approves."

"He's not shy about his opinions, Glory. If he didn't approve, he'd have let me know."

"What if it doesn't work out? What if you find out you really like your privacy and you don't want to have someone sharing your space twenty-four-seven?"

We pulled to the curb in front of Southern Treasures. Jake turned off the engine and turned in the seat to face me. "Glory, I'm not a kid; I know what I want and I am not going to change my mind. But if we have issues, I think we can find solutions. That's what couples do. That's what Karen and Riley are doing, in case you hadn't noticed. And that's what we would do."

When I didn't answer, he continued. "If you're really worried about Bluebeard, you can stay here tonight and make arrangements to take him to my place at night."

"I'll stay here, too, if you want."

"How can you? Everything's torn up, and I don't have a kitchen; I can't even make coffee in the morning, much less something resembling breakfast." My voice cracked as tears stung my eyes. It was all just too much.

"Hey, there's a bed to sleep in, a shower with hot water, and the best coffee in town right downstairs. What more do I need?"

He stretched awkwardly across the console to hug me. "Besides you, of course."

That was all it took. The stress of watching my home torn apart, the shock of Fowler's death, and the horror of what Jake had heard about how he died? I could handle all that.

But Jake's tenderness and support? That was the last straw.

Jake held me while I cried, but the waterworks didn't last long. Just knowing I could break down, that there was a safe place to let go, helped calm me. It took only a minute or two for the storm of emotions to pass.

I looked up at him in the faint glow of the streetlights.

"Are you going to leave the car here, or park it behind your bookstore?"

"How about I park it around back and move it in the morning? Right now I don't want to let you out of my sight."

"I'm fine," I sniffled. "Just stressed out and tired, with another long day tomorrow. If you're really okay with the disaster area, let's go upstairs and call if a night."

Jake was smart enough not to argue with me. He pulled the car around the block and tucked it into the small space behind the store, next to my vintage pickup.

The sight of the truck lifted my spirits, as it always did. I'd "bought" it from Sly a few years earlier, though the price I'd paid made it more of a gift, and I would always be grateful.

Once inside the back door I reset the alarms before heading into the store to check on Bluebeard before going upstairs. Best to let him know I was home before he made trouble.

Too late.

If I didn't know better, I would have thought someone had vandalized the shop. But I'd seen this before. Bluebeard expressed his displeasure by rearranging the shop, with disastrous results.

Two quilts that should have been hanging on the wall draped over the case of vintage jewelry. Wadded up T-shirts littered the floor underneath the clothing rack. Glassware, though still on the shelves, no longer stood in neat rows.

The real point, however, was on the front counter: pages of vintage copies of the *Keyhole News and Times* covered the counter, each one spread open to a specific page.

I'd learned what that meant when Uncle Louis first revealed himself; something important was on those pages and he wanted me to find it.

I wondered once again what the rules were for ghosts. If he could speak to me through Bluebeard, why did he have to resort to dragging old newspapers onto the counter? How did he even know I needed whatever information he was showing me? Why couldn't he just *tell* me what I needed to know?

And what did he want tell me this time?

CHAPTER 12

I heard Jake's sharp intake of breath behind me.

"It's just Bluebeard," I assured him. "This is why I don't like to leave him alone for too long."

He gave a low whistle. "You've told me he does this," he said. "But I didn't realize how much mess he made."

I turned on the overhead lights, all hope of an early evening abandoned. "It really isn't that bad. He never damages anything, just throws stuff around and pushes things onto the floor.

"You'll notice," I continued, picking up shirts from the floor, "that he didn't knock down any glass, the expensive quits aren't on the floor, and the shirts are still on the hangers."

I swiftly sorted the shirts back into their proper places on the rack. Jake, without prompting, gathered the quilts and carefully hung them back on the wall.

It took another twenty minutes to put everything back in place and realign the rows of glasses. Bluebeard remained silently in his cage throughout the process, though we made enough noise that he had to be awake.

I glanced over the newspapers, wondering exactly which articles I was supposed to see. That much could wait until morning. After a night's sleep, I would have a better chance of unraveling the puzzle Bluebeard had left for me.

Jake joined me at the counter, and started to refold the newspapers.

"Don't!"

He looked at me, startled.

"Sorry. I didn't mean to sound so sharp. It's just that I know I'm supposed to read something on those pages. That's how he's done it in the past."

He raised his eyebrows, unvoiced questions evident in his expression.

"I know, I know," I said, shaking my head. "Sounds crazy. But he's done this before. There's something he wants to tell me, and instead of just *telling* me he leaves things thrown around for me to find."

"Ooookay," Jake dragged out the word as though trying to believe it really was okay.

"I get it. Really. I don't know why he won't just say whatever it is. Instead I get these clues that I have to try and figure out, which takes way longer," my voice was rising with the frustration I felt.

"Trying to $&$*^%$#(* sleep."

Finally Bluebeard saw fit to respond.

"So was I," I shot back. "Until someone decided to trash my shop."

"I'm helping," he sing-songed from inside the cage.

"Not really," I muttered. Turning to Jake I continued, "Let's go upstairs. I'll look at the papers in the morning."

Exhausted, and surrounded by the chaos that used to be my apartment, I fell into bed far later than I had planned.

THE SMELL of strong coffee tickled my nose, teasing me from sleep. For one sweet moment I was back in my cozy home, the coffee brewing in the kitchen as I drifted awake.

Then the moment evaporated into reality. I was home, in my no-longer-cozy apartment. I had no kitchen, there was no coffee brewing, and I still had a mess to finish cleaning downstairs.

There was, however, Jake.

Jake, who had managed to get up without waking me, and who was now standing next to the bed with a large to-go cup from Lighthouse. That explained the heavenly smell.

I pushed myself into a sitting position. Jake handed me my cup and retrieved his from the top of the dresser.

"Figured you could use that," he said with a grin.

"You have no idea." I sipped carefully, judging the heat before taking a large swallow.

I glanced at the clock. Too early for Lighthouse to even be open. I looked back at Jake, sitting on the edge of the bed.

"What can I say?" he answered the question in my gaze. "I was awake so I went down to the kitchen and told Chloe the boss needed coffee. She was happy to help me out. Said if we came down in thirty minutes there would be fresh quiche for breakfast."

He shrugged. "She knows you don't have a kitchen right now. Besides, I think she likes to show off her cooking."

I sighed with contentment. I could get used to being awakened by fresh coffee delivered by my own personal waiter. As long as that waiter was Jake.

But there wasn't time for lolling around drinking coffee. If Chloe was promising quiche in thirty minutes, I needed to get moving. Especially since I still had to make time to deal with the newspapers I'd left on the counter last night.

"Shower," I said, hanging my legs over the side of the bed. I stood up, grabbed my coffee, and headed for the bathroom. "Give me ten minutes," I called over my shoulder before closing the door.

It was closer to fifteen, but by the time I was dressed the coffee was working its magic. I checked the time and gestured toward the stairs. "We've got a few minutes," I said. "I should go feed Bluebeard before we go eat. Although he shouldn't get any treats after the mess he made last night."

"What was that about?" Jake asked as he followed me down the stairs. "Does he do that whenever you stay out?"

I stopped halfway down and thought about his question. "No," I answered after a moment, "not all the time, anyway. Sometimes he pushes a shirt on the floor, or moves a glass, or drags down a quilt.

"But he's only done the newspaper trick a couple times. And only when he wanted to tell me something important."

At the bottom of the stairs, I stopped to retrieve some melon from the small refrigerator. Mess or not, he had to eat.

I scanned the shelves as I made my way past them to Bluebeard's cage. Nothing seemed disturbed since we'd put things to right the night before. I breathed a sigh of relief and gave Bluebeard his breakfast while Jake refilled his water.

"Pretty boy," Bluebeard said sweetly, as though he hadn't been a complete brat just a few hours earlier.

"Don't sweet talk me," Jake told him. "I'm not the one you need to apologize to."

Bluebeard laughed, a sound eerily similar to the toddler giggle of Rose Ann, Julie's daughter.

"That's not an apology, old man." I put the food dish in front of him. "But I know better than to expect one from you."

Still, I couldn't stay mad at him. I gave him pets and hand-fed him a couple pieces of melon before leaving him to finish on his own.

I crossed back to the counter, carefully stacking the spread-out newspapers to keep them in order and open to the proper page.

"Come on," I said to Jake, picking up the stack of papers. "Let's go get breakfast. We can look at these while we eat."

Jake took the papers from me while I turned off the alarm and unlocked the connecting door. I was locking it behind us when I heard another squawk from Bluebeard.

"Watch out for woman trouble!"

This time he refused to repeat himself and we were left to puzzle out his cryptic message for ourselves.

"Any idea what that was about?" Jake asked.

"No. And it isn't the first time he's said that."

Lighthouse Coffee wasn't open for another few minutes, but Chloe was expecting us. "Your breakfast is almost ready. If you sit back here," she gestured to a table against the wall, "no one will see you and expect me to let them in."

She looked quizzically at the pile of newspapers in Jake's hands, but when we didn't offer an explanation, she didn't pry.

A carafe of fresh coffee and two heavy diner-style mugs were already on the table, so we pulled another table over to hold the papers. No sense chancing a spill.

"There are no marks on these pages," Jake said, examining the paper from the top of the stack. "If he did this, how did he not tear them?"

I noticed he avoided using Bluebeard's name.

I shook my head. "I thought the same thing, the first time this happened. I have no idea how, I just know he did."

Chloe delivered our food, made sure we had everything we needed, and disappeared back to the kitchen with a promise to check on us later. "Still have some baking to finish before we open," she said.

The quiche was delicious, but my curiosity overcame my hunger and I scooted toward the second table after just a few bites.

The date on the first paper was October 9, 1989. I scanned the page, wondering which of the articles held Bluebeard's clue. Meeting notices? I didn't think the Ladies Quilting Circle at the Baptist church, a city council meeting, or the discreet mention of a gathering of "friends of Bill" had anything to do with "woman trouble."

Assuming the papers and Bluebeard's warning even had a connection, which wasn't guaranteed.

I said as much to Jake.

"We have to start somewhere," he said. "So let's assume that they are. If we don't find anything, then we look again."

I nodded. "It's as good a starting point as any."

We examined the rest of the page, eliminating several other small articles.

A name jumped out at me from an announcement just below the fold on the second page.

Fowler.

I nudged Jake and pointed at the item. "Mr. and Mrs. Matthew Fowler are pleased to announce the arrival of their son, Joseph McKenzie Fowler," I read softly.

The announcement went on to list the grandparents and great-grandparents as well as the baby's vital statistics, and identified his father as a "prominent businessman and civic leader in Keyhole Bay."

"I wonder how much he had to pay for that," Jake said.

"Probably nothing. He's always been a good customer of the *News and Times*, buys lots of advertising. That'll make you prominent in the eyes of the paper."

He looked up at me and I rolled my eyes. "It's a small town and he's one of the good ol' boys," I reminded him.

I carefully folded the paper, leaving the birth announcement exposed, and set it aside. "For now let's assume that's significant."

"What's next?"

The next issue was April of the same year. Assuming we were right about the previous article, we didn't need to guess this time. Half the page was coverage of the marriage of Matthew Archibald Fowler and Karoline Rose Fitzgerald McKenzie.

Jake read the name aloud and gave me a questioning look. "Really?"

I snickered. "The family has always claimed they are related to her. Just like the Andersons at Back Bay Bank claimed they were related to General Anderson.

"I don't believe this one either, but I suppose anything's possible."

The wedding story went on for paragraph after paragraph, describing the bride's gown, the flowers, and dozens of details of the parties and showers leading up to the ceremony.

I was still reading the article when Jake began to chuckle.

"What?" I said.

"Look at the date," he said, grinning.

"April 2, 1989." I shrugged. "At least it wasn't April Fool's Day, though that might have been appropriate."

"That's not it. April to," he gestured to the previous article, "October? Looks like little Joe arrived a bit early."

I grinned back at him. "Wonder what Kerrie's namesake would have to say about that?"

"Nothing good, I'm sure," he replied. "And this sounds like woman trouble to me."

CHAPTER 13

*C*hloe came through a few minutes later, turned on the OPEN sign in the front window, and came to check on us.

"Breakfast okay?" she asked, eyeing our half-finished plates.

"It's delicious," Jake assured her. "As always. We just got distracted with some reading."

"Do you want me to heat it back up?" she asked, reaching for his plate.

"No need," he said, waving her hand away. "It's just fine the way it is."

"Sure?" She withdrew her hand, but her face was clouded with doubt.

I took a quick look around. We were still alone, though that likely wouldn't last long.

"Want to join us for a few minutes?" I asked, gesturing to a chair at the next table.

Chloe hesitated. I was her boss now, not just the woman who owned the shop next door, and we were still working out how that affected our relationship. I wished it didn't—I'd always liked Chloe—but buying Lighthouse Coffee made it inevitable.

"Sit down," I said with a smile. "I'll show you what is keeping me from this delicious quiche."

She dragged a chair over, grabbed a mug for coffee, and joined us at our improvised conference table.

"You know what happened to Matt Fowler?" The question was rhetorical. Gossip was a major industry in Keyhole Bay, a close second to tourism, and well ahead of fishing and T-shirt shops. Of course she knew; at least she knew as much as anyone did.

Except, perhaps, Uncle Louis.

"It's terrible! I talked to Shiloh for a few minutes yesterday. You know Joe was the one who found him?" Shiloh Weaver was the former office manager for Fowler Auto Sales, and the mention of her name reminded me that she and Joe Fowler—Matt's only child—had become a public item after Shiloh quit working at the dealership. The relationship had started well before then, though they'd tried to keep it quiet.

I shook my head. "I just heard it was a 'family member.'" Jake's friends had thought it was Fowler's son. Now we had confirmation. "How awful."

"She wasn't able to say much about the accident, just that she'd hardly seen Joe since because he's busy taking care of his mom, and when she does see him, he is just a total wreck."

She shrugged. "Which totally makes sense, you know? I mean, he found his dad with a car on top of him. That's got to be pretty messed up."

I felt a momentary flash of amusement at her analysis. She was a psych major at Keyhole Bay Community College, though she'd cut back her class load when she started managing Lighthouse. Usually her assessment of someone's emotional state was a bit more clinical than *pretty messed up*.

The amusement faded as quickly as it came though. There was nothing amusing about what had happened to Fowler, or the emotional fallout that was now raining down on his family.

I noticed, too, that Chloe called it an accident. "Did Shiloh say it was an accident?" I asked. "I really hadn't heard much about what happened."

I usually wasn't a very good liar, and I hoped I wouldn't give myself away. But Chloe had at least talked to Shiloh, and that was as close as I was going to get to any more real information for the moment.

"Yeah. She wasn't supposed to tell me—I don't think Joe was supposed to tell her—but Joe said his dad was working on his car and something went wrong."

More confirmation of what Jake had overheard.

She paused. "But what has that got to do with breakfast?" she asked, pulling the conversation back to safer, and less upsetting, territory.

"Well, I was looking at some old newspapers this morning, and I found a couple things about the Fowlers." I gestured to the papers spread out on the table. "It was just strange to see this," I showed her the page with the wedding announcement, "after what happened. You look at things differently, you know?"

Chloe nodded solemnly.

I braced myself, afraid she would ask why I was looking at the papers. Before she could, though, the front door opened to admit the first customers of the morning and Chloe excused herself to wait on them.

"Saved by the bell," Jake said softly as she walked away.

"Literally," I replied. "And she knew some things we didn't. Like confirming that Joe was the one who found him, and the family seems to believe it was an accident.

"Even if Bluebeard doesn't."

More customers came in, so I relinquished the second table, carefully gathering the newspapers into a neat pile to take back to the store.

We finished out breakfast and Jake carried our dishes to the counter so Chloe wouldn't have to clear the table. Judging by the line growing at the counter, she wouldn't be getting to it any time soon.

Although I opened late on Sunday mornings, I still had a lot of paperwork to do, so I let Jake out the back door to retrieve his car and settled myself behind the counter.

Buying out my cousin Peter's portion of Southern Treasures had been the best decision I'd ever made, but buying Lighthouse Coffee at the same time had generated a massive amount of bookkeeping. I still found myself falling behind and continually having to struggle to catch up. I told myself the extra hours this morning were the answer to my prayers.

Now I was even lying to myself.

CHAPTER 14

*B*luebeard behaved himself through the day, entertaining the children and flirting with the women, his antics encouraging the sales of T-shirts and mugs with his likeness on them.

He drew people in, and I couldn't believe my cousin Peter had wanted me to bar him from the shop for liability reasons. One of the many reasons I'd been glad to buy Peter's share of the business. I was still paying him off, but another good summer and the place would be all mine.

Well, mine and the bank's. Fortunately, the bank was proving to be a better partner than Peter had ever been.

I still had a couple more newspapers to examine, but by the time I was ready to close for the day, I was too restless to sit still long enough to focus.

I turned off the "Open" sign and bribed Bluebeard with a shredded-wheat biscuit. "Be right back," I told him. "Just going next door for a couple minutes."

"Coffee?"

I shook my head. "No coffee. You know better. Besides, I'm not going to Lighthouse."

I locked the door behind me and went to the left, toward the Grog

Shop. There was one person in Keyhole Bay I could ask about Matthew Fowler and count on a straight answer—Linda Miller.

Linda and her husband owned the Grog Shop next to Southern Treasures. My former babysitter, she was a cross between an adopted mom and the older sister I never had. Linda and Guy took me in when my folks died, and she was the one person I trusted more than anyone else in my life.

Besides, her younger sister had some history with Fowler over money, and that just might mean "woman trouble" of a very different kind.

A line of tourists stood at the counter, buying snacks and sodas for the trip home. A few carried stronger stuff, likely heading home to a dry county or one where blue laws kept them from buying alcohol on Sunday.

I waved to Linda, who was running the register with practiced ease, and headed into the storage area. As I expected, Guy was loading a hand truck with cases of beer for the cooler. I gave him a hand, falling easily into a routine we'd had since I was too young to actually sell the stuff.

"You close early?" he asked, stacking a final case on the hand truck.

"Not really." I opened the walk-in cooler while he maneuvered the heavy load around the crowd of customers.

"That late already?" he said, heaving cases onto the shelves. "Time flies when you're having fun."

I grinned at him as I hefted cases into place. "I am not sure you know what fun means."

By the time we finished restocking the walk-in, Linda had taken care of the line at the counter and was closing up.

"Good weekend?" I asked as she ran the register reports for the end of day.

She nodded. "Pretty fair. How about you?"

We compared notes on the weekend's business as she finished her calculations and emptied the till. She carried the bank bag toward the back and I followed along while she stashed it in the safe and locked the back doors.

"There was something I wanted to ask you about," I said.

"I figured."

Guy appeared in the doorway. "Ready?" he asked his wife.

"Just about."

I looked from one to the other. "You hungry? I'm thinking about a burger, my treat."

"You must really want something," Linda said. "But if it means I don't have to cook, I'm in."

"How about The Tank?" I suggested. The fisherman's bar near the docks had the best tavern food in town. "Meet you there in about fifteen minutes? I just need to grab my purse and check in with Jake."

"Check in with Jake?" Guy asked. He sounded like a dad checking up on his daughter's date, and it made me smile. I might be a grown woman, but he was still looking out for me. Fortunately for me, he and Linda both liked Jake a lot.

"Make sure he's ready to eat," I corrected, still grinning.

Twenty minutes later, the four of us were gathered around a scarred wood table in the back of the bar.

Outside, the fishing boats drifted silently in their moorings, their catch off-loaded early in the afternoon and their crews gone home to their families. Later the place would fill with the crew from the processing facility, but for now, the place was empty except for a couple of captains swapping lies over a beer at the bar.

I waited until we placed our orders, then turned to Linda. I wasn't sure where to start, so I plunged right in.

"You know what happened to Matt Fowler, right?" It wasn't really a question; everyone in town had talked of nothing else for days, and I was sure she and Guy had heard every rumor.

She nodded for me to go ahead.

"It's got Bluebeard upset. Again." Linda and Guy had known about Uncle Louis almost as long as I had. I didn't need to explain what I meant.

"Upset how?" she asked.

"He's been telling me to watch out for 'woman trouble,'" I used my fingers to put air quotes around the words, "and last night when I came home, he'd messed up the store."

Linda's shocked expression made me hurry ahead. "Nothing was damaged, just some stuff out of place. You know how he does, just getting my attention."

"Except the newspapers," Jake added darkly.

"Yes, but they weren't ripped or anything. Just spread on the counter, open to specific articles." I looked down at the table and kind of mumbled. "Like he did before."

"Like *what?*" Guy asked.

"Like he did before," I repeated in a low voice. I hadn't told them everything, but now I had to explain how I'd found relevant newspapers spread on the counter several times over the last few years.

"But how can it be the parrot?" Guy continued his questioning. "How can he move newspapers without tearing them with his claws or his beak? That isn't even possible."

I shook my head. "I have no idea. I mean, how does he say the things he does? How does he know the stuff he does? I have no idea how any of this works.

"I just know that he's done this before, and he's doing it again. And it seems to be about this Fowler business."

Jake and I explained the articles we'd read that morning, pausing while the waitress delivered our round of burgers.

"I didn't have time to look at the rest," I said around a bite of burger. "But you can bet they're going to be the same kind of thing— more old stories about the Fowler family."

I ate in silence for a minute, letting Guy and Linda digest what I'd just told them, before I finally asked the question that had been on my mind all day.

"So what I wanted to ask was, what do you know about Fowler and his family? Not the stuff we all know, like how he's such a pillar of the community, and a big deal in the Booster Club and the Merchant's Association. Or even the stuff we've all heard, about why Kerrie gets a new car every couple years or those diamonds she wears."

Guy gave a disgusted snort, clearly expressing his opinion of the Fowlers and their relationship.

Linda hesitated, looking guilty.

"You *do* know something, don't you?" I didn't exactly pounce on her, but I wanted to know. "Is it the stuff about the prom fund? About Annie's trouble with him? Could that be the 'woman trouble' Bluebeard is talking about?"

Her eyes widened and she sat a little straighter. "What do you know about that? *How* do you know about that? Nobody was supposed to know." She colored slightly. "Even me."

"But your little sister had to tell somebody, didn't she?"

She glanced at Guy, who looked as mystified as Jake did. "Yes, she did. But I never breathed a word to anyone. There's no way you could know. And I really don't think it could be what Bluebeard is talking about. There was an issue, yes, but it was just about money, nothing personal."

"I won't tell you how I know." I couldn't reveal that Karen had heard a rumor from a colleague who'd been over-celebrating his retirement. "But I do know there was some scandal about the prom fund when Annie was the treasurer, and it got covered up."

I sat back and waited while Linda absorbed the news that Annie's secret wasn't so secret after all. It took her a couple minutes, but I could see the moment when she decided she didn't have to stay silent about Fowler's misdeed any longer.

She leaned forward, talking quietly. We all leaned in too, listening carefully.

"I promised Annie I would never tell another soul what happened," she said. "And I'm not real happy sharing this, but it's probably time somebody knows the truth."

"We're not going to repeat it," I assured her. "And several people already know."

"I know. Still..." Her voice trailed off and for a minute I thought she was going to stop. Then she took a deep breath and started talking.

Her story confirmed the few details I already knew. Matthew Fowler had somehow managed to get his name on the bank account for the Junior-Senior Prom the year Annie was Treasurer. Sometime after Christmas, Annie found money missing from the account. Fowler admitted to her he had withdrawn the funds, he replaced them immediately, and the entire matter was covered up.

"One thing I don't understand," I said after she laid out the basics. "Why was his name on the account? Annie was only a couple years ahead of me, so he must have been out of school by then, right? If I remember the dates in the newspaper, he was already married and had a kid."

Linda confirmed my timeline. "He'd been out of school a few years. Went away to college, but only for a year. As soon as he came back, he set up a used car lot and started working his way into the Merchant's Association and the Booster Club and a bunch of other civic groups. It was like he set out to make himself a big name around town. And he succeeded."

I thought about the birth announcement that described him as a prominent businessman. Whatever he'd done had definitely succeeded, and rather quickly.

"Back then we'd only been married a few years," Guy said, "and we were trying to buy the Grog Shop."

His normally calm demeanor showed cracks, and he looked almost angry. "For a while it looked like Fowler was going to outbid us—he already had his first car lot and he was looking to branch out, 'diversi-fy,' he said, but his liquor license got held up and he finally had to give up. He couldn't make the deal without an approved license applica-tion. Now that I hear about this situation with Annie, I have to wonder if the two things were related."

"I never knew that." Linda sounded shocked that Guy had never told her that story.

"I'd forgotten it myself," Guy said. "Until just this minute. At the time I didn't want to worry you, then once he couldn't get the license it just wasn't important, and then we were so busy getting the store running and trying to keep our heads above water that I never even thought about it." He reached out and squeezed her hand. "Sorry, hon."

She shrugged and squeezed back. "Well, I didn't tell you about the thing with Annie, so I guess we're kind of even."

Linda turned back to me. "Anyway, he had wormed his way into some kind of advisory position with the high school student council, even though he was only a few years older than the students he was supposed to be advising."

"Was Kerrie one of those students?" Jake asked.

She thought for a minute, then shook her head. "Could have been. I was trying to remember but I'm not sure. He dated a lot of women during that time."

Guy laughed. "Sure did. Seemed to like being known around town as an eligible bachelor. I guess some of the women thought he was a good catch."

"The ones without a lick of sense," Linda muttered.

"As for Kerrie, she graduated just the year before they got married," Linda said, furrowing her brow as she concentrated on twenty-five-year-old memories. "And I think I remember hearing some talk that he'd met her while he was on the advisory council."

She made a face. "Nothing wrong with that, I guess. He was only a couple years older than she was. Still..." She let her voice trail off, clearly uncomfortable with the turn the conversation had taken.

"And Joe was born about six months after they got married?" I asked.

"That caused some talk," Linda admitted, answering the unvoiced part of my question. "But it wasn't that big a deal since they were already married. Not like it might have been a few years before."

"So now he's married, has a kid, has his car lot," I summarized. "*And* he's running around trying to be important, and gets caught with his hand in the cookie jar. Right so far?"

"Yes." Linda started again, now brisk and businesslike. "According to Annie, he never actually said why he took the money, or what he intended to do with it, but he was able to repay it immediately. She said he even made a contribution to the fund that was more than they would have earned in interest if it was in the bank, which was part of why no one raised a fuss about what he'd done.

"Kind of a 'no harm, no foul' thing. He resigned from the advisory committee, claiming the new baby and the business kept him too busy. Everybody took his explanation at face value, and the couple people that might have known about what he'd done kept quiet.

"Annie let it drop, said nobody'd believe her, she was just a 16-year-old kid, and she'd gone directly to him as the fund's advisor when she noticed the missing funds so he was able to cover it up before anyone else could get involved. I think she might have talked to somebody on the faculty, but if she did, nothing ever came of it.

"That fall Fowler started focusing in earnest on the Booster Club, and y'all know how that worked for him."

"Yeah," I said, sarcasm tingeing my voice. "Right up to the point where one of his employees killed the star quarterback."

Guy nodded. "But nothing stuck to *him* over that, you'll notice. It was like he was made of Teflon."

Jake sat back a little, looking thoughtful. "Let me get this straight. Kerrie was maybe still a student when he met her. He was dating lots of other women at the time, playing at being an eligible bachelor, but he obviously got involved with her at some point.

"He married Kerrie less than a year after she graduated, and Joe came along six months later."

He looked around the table and sat up even straighter.

"That all adds up to 'woman trouble' in my book."

CHAPTER 15

*J*ake and I ended up back at my apartment. Moving Bluebeard between Jake's house and the store just seemed like one more complication to deal with, and I already had way too much on my plate for one day.

"I'll try to figure it out tomorrow, when Julie's here."

Jake reluctantly agreed, reminding me that we would have to cook at his place on Thursday, since it was my night to host dinner. My answering groan was greeted with a told-you-so grin, which I tried to ignore.

"Can't we just have pizza?" I whined.

"We could. You make a pretty mean pizza, as I recall. But I'd be glad to put on a pot of spaghetti or chili or something."

I laughed in spite of myself. "Firehouse food, right?"

Jake's sheepish chuckle confirmed my suspicion. "Even after all these years away, I still fall back on what I know when I'm cooking for a crowd," he admitted.

"You call six people a crowd?" I asked. "Most of the people I knew would call it a family dinner."

Sure, they might not have that many immediate family living at home, but there were always kids and grandkids and extended family nearby.

Besides, in our small town family had a rather loose definition and often included anyone who was around at mealtime. And those of us without families of blood collected our own families of the heart, as I had with Karen and Riley, Felipe and Ernie, and Jake.

And Uncle Louis.

"Not in my family," Jake said. I knew he had just one brother and a couple nieces he saw only occasionally.

"Nor mine," I admitted. "But there was always someone extra for supper."

"Seems like smaller families are more common now, though."

I thought about it, and had to admit he was right.

For some reason, probably because he'd been on my mind for the last several days, I thought of Matthew Fowler. Joe was his only child, just as I had been an only child.

I wondered how Joe was holding up. I'd met him once or twice at the dealership and my initial impression, before I knew who he was, had been less than favorable. Later I realized he was just a young man trying to impress an overbearing and demanding father, with little success. A little understanding went a long way toward changing that first impression.

Now he would never have the chance. Would that make it better, or worse? The constant pressure must be difficult; on the other hand, he might always have "unfinished business." I certainly had, but most 17-year-olds did. Would it be different for someone in his 20s?

I pushed the thoughts aside and got ready for bed. Whatever Joe Fowler's problems were, I had plenty of my own to keep me occupied. No sense in borrowing trouble.

Later, drifting off to sleep with Jake snoring softly next to me, my mind wandered back to the question of Matthew Fowler. I still couldn't imagine how it happened.

He was a jerk, but he paid attention to details and he wouldn't have tolerated a malfunctioning piece of machinery. At the very least, he'd have been on the phone to the maintenance company insisting they fix it immediately.

One other thing occurred to me before I nodded off: The only times Bluebeard had been this upset were murders. So why was he so upset over an accident?

By the time Jake and I wandered downstairs the next morning in search of coffee and quiche, I had convinced myself there was more to Fowler's death. Bluebeard's reaction alone would have been enough; with the other questions, I simply couldn't accept Boomer's initial assessment.

I said as much to Jake when we were settled at our table in the back of the shop.

"Boomer isn't telling us anything," I said around a savory bite of eggs stuffed with bacon and Swiss cheese. "He hasn't even released a cause of death, as far as I know."

"Did you expect him to call you with that information?" Jake asked.

I glanced up and caught a grin that told me he was teasing, but I had to admit he had a point.

"No." I washed down my quiche with a big sip of cafe au lait laced with chicory. Pansy might shudder at the addition to her menu, but the New Orleans treat was proving popular with the tourists and locals alike.

And with me.

"But you'd think he would be anxious to get this situation settled and put it behind him. After all, Fowler was kind of a big deal."

Jake shrugged. "Big deal or not, no public official wants to jump the gun and then be wrong. It's a lot worse than delaying, even when people are badgering you for an answer."

There was a note of resigned authority in his voice, as though he knew exactly what he was talking about. He had been a public official before his forced retirement from the fire department back in California, and I suspected he was speaking from experience. I made a mental note to ask him about it in private.

"You really think he's getting badgered?"

"You think Freed isn't bugging him?" he shot back, quirking one eyebrow in disbelief.

I had to nod my agreement. Karen wouldn't let go of the story until she had her answers, and if that meant leaning on Boomer every chance she got—well, that was exactly what she would do.

I was about to head next door to open up Southern Treasures when Chloe threaded her way through the tables of customers, her eyes wide, her mouth a tiny, shocked "o," and the line at the counter momentarily forgotten.

I didn't have to ask if anything was wrong; it clearly was.

But I would have never guessed what it was, or how very wrong.

CHAPTER 16

"Shiloh just called me. I think she might need a friend. Any chance you could cover for a little while?"

I shook my head. "I'll need time to call Julie to cover the shop since it's her day off.

"What's wrong?"

"Joe." She said it as though the one word was all I needed. It explained everything and nothing. Shiloh and Matthew Fowler's son had been a thing for a couple years, ever since she quit working for his father. Or maybe before she quit, if local gossip was to be believed. Either way, I could understand her concern over Joe, but it had been several days. Why was Shiloh suddenly so distressed?

My puzzlement must have shown on my face, because Chloe did a double take and unleashed a torrent of words. "It's not Joe exactly, it's his mom. Well, not even his mom. It's the lawyer."

I shot a glance at Jake, who looked as confused as I felt. Clearly this wasn't making any sense to him, either.

"His mother's lawyer?" Jake asked. "What could Clifford Wilson have done to upset Kerrie? Hasn't he been their lawyer for decades?"

"Not him." Chloe shook her head. "Let me try this again. Shiloh is worried about Joe and she kind of needs a shoulder right now. Kerrie is pitching a hissy fit about the will, and that lawyer from Tallahassee is telling her she can't do anything until his client agrees."

Tallahassee?" I parroted.

"His client?" Jake asked.

"The first wife," Chloe explained. "She's saying her son has the right to half the estate, and Kerrie can't do anything until that claim is settled."

I sat back in my chair. Stunned didn't begin to describe how I felt. Matthew Fowler had a first wife? And she had a son? And she thought they had a claim to Fowler's estate?

No wonder the Fowler family—and, by extension, Shiloh—was in a tizzy.

I had never heard about Fowler being married before Kerrie. He'd lived in Keyhole Bay his entire life, except for that one year of college, so when did he even have time for another wife and son? And I would bet no one else had heard any of this, either.

Including Kerrie.

Jake was on his feet immediately. "Go," he told Chloe. "I'll go open the store until Glory can call Julie. I don't have to open the bookstore for a couple hours."

Chloe ripped off her apron and shot me a questioning look. When I didn't object, she ran out the through the kitchen. I heard the back door slam shut behind her.

Jake looked at me, a frown creasing his brow. "Sorry," he shook his head. "Sometimes in an emergency I forget I'm not in charge anymore."

"It's okay," I said automatically.

Jake hesitated for a second, then gave me a quick kiss. "I promised I'd open the store. I better go feed Bluebeard and make sure he hasn't gotten into any more trouble." He nodded toward the counter. "Unless you want me to make coffee?"

I considered his offer for about a nanosecond.

"Get an apron," I said. "I'll call Julie."

As I went next door to use the phone, I wondered if I had really meant what I said. Was it really okay that he had just assumed control of my employee and my business? If it was, what did that say about our relationship?

For that matter, what did it say about me?

I shook off the moment of introspection.

I could think about that later. Right now I needed to call Julie to cover the store.

That was easier said than done. I had to leave voice mail and wait three-quarters of an hour for her to call back, only to find that she had plans she couldn't change.

"I'm sorry, Glory. Really I am! But we had to wait a month for Rose Ann's pediatrician to have an opening, so I can't reschedule."

She was right, of course. Rose Ann was her first priority and I wouldn't have it any other way. But it didn't stop me from feeling sorry for myself. I'd have to spend the day running back and forth, or close down either the souvenir shop or the bakery, and I didn't like any of those options.

When I told Jake that Julie couldn't come in and I was going to have to call Chloe back in, he opened his mouth and instantly shut it again. "Not my business, not my call," he said after pausing for a second.

I hesitated. Maybe this was one of those things we needed to work out, just as Karen and Riley were doing.

I trusted Jake's judgment, and I needed to make that clear.

"I'd like to hear what you think." I held up a hand to stop his answer. "Let me finish."

He nodded.

"I'd like your advice, but I reserve the right not to follow it. Either way, the choice is mine.

"Fair enough?"

Silence stretched like taffy on the rollers in the candy shop window. A few seconds felt like an hour, as though everything hung in the balance.

I didn't have a lot of experience with this relationship stuff. Maybe I'd just blown it completely.

MURDER BUYS A LEMON

Jake smiled slowly. "Good. Just keep reminding me if I forget who's the boss here."

A protest rose to my lips. I wanted to tell him I wasn't the boss, but the words died before I could speak because he was right. When it came to Lighthouse and Southern Treasures, I was the boss and I needed to act like it.

Outside of the stores might be a different matter, and that was something we would have to figure out. But in here, yes, I was the boss.

"So let's hear it," I prodded him. "What's your idea?"

"Janey's due in at noon," he said. "She can handle Beach Books by herself for the afternoon. Open Southern Treasures a little late and I'll take care of the shop while you work over here."

I turned the plan over in my brain for a couple minutes, but couldn't find any major flaws. Sure, it meant leaving Southern Treasures closed for the morning, but at least I wouldn't lose the whole day.

"Can you take care of Bluebeard before you go open up?" I asked, glancing pointedly at the line beginning to form at the counter after a brief lull.

"Sure thing." He started toward the shop next door, throwing the last word over his shoulder. "Boss."

I took just a moment to watch him walk away—it was a nice view —before I stepped up to the counter and started serving customers.

It felt like something had just fallen into place, but I didn't have time to examine it right now. Right now I had hungry customers to take care of.

I served my customers, but my speed and coordination couldn't match Chloe's. She earned her designation as godsend every day, as the growing line made me acutely aware.

I must have looked as desperate as I felt, because when Karen came through the door late in the morning she immediately came around the counter.

She eyed the line of go-cups arrayed in front of me at the espresso machine, scanned the scrawled tickets on the counter, and started pulling pastries from the case and matching them to the tickets.

I shot her what I hoped was a look of gratitude and went back to pulling shots, steaming milk, and pumping syrup. Making coffee was a time-consuming process and I marveled at the idea that Chloe managed it by herself every morning.

The line quickly became visibly shorter, and I sighed with relief. Maybe I would survive this morning after all. Within a few minutes, Karen had taken the last order and served the last pastry, giving me a chance to catch up on the coffee orders.

At last I turned to her, my shoulders unclenching for the first time since Chloe had made her announcement and run out.

"What can I get you?" I said, as though she hadn't asked that same question a dozen times herself.

She laughed. "Coffee. Black. Don't want to work you to death. And I'll get my own muffin."

We stood behind the counter in case another wave of customers appeared, but for the moment, things were calm.

"So what are you doing over here?" Karen asked. "Shouldn't you be next door?" She glanced toward the recently-installed door that connected Lighthouse's kitchen with Southern Treasures' warehouse.

I gave her a brief recap of Chloe's departure.

"Jake did what?! No. Never mind that. For now. But repeat what you said about a wife. Fowler had another wife?"

"A first wife is what Chloe said. And it sure sounded like it was a surprise to Kerrie."

I thought back to the newspapers Bluebeard had spread across the counter on Saturday night. They were still stacked in the warehouse where we'd left them after yesterday's breakfast. I wondered if anything in them would hint at Fowler's hidden second family.

"Maybe," I said softly, "that's the woman trouble Bluebeard's been talking about. Not Kerrie, or Linda's sister, but this other wife. What-ever her name is."

"Woman trouble?"

"He's said it a couple times." Might as well go for broke. "And he's done the newspaper thing again."

Karen's eyes widened. She knew the significance of "the newspaper thing," had seen it for herself. "Any idea what he's trying to tell you?"

I shrugged. "Not for sure. But so far, all the articles I found seem to relate to Fowler."

Once again I thought of how Bluebeard had only become upset when murder was involved.

Maybe that was what he was trying to tell me. That Fowler's death wasn't an accident.

Or maybe I was letting my imagination run away with me.

Before I could ask Karen what she thought, a couple came through the front door with a stroller. I tried not to stare at what was obviously the ugliest child I had ever seen. It took my brain several seconds to register that it wasn't a child at all, but a small, pink piglet.

While I considered several ways to deal with the situation, Karen went into reporter mode. She whipped around the counter and drew the couple aside, asking them questions about their, well, pig, as she guide them back onto the sidewalk.

Seconds later she stuck her head back in and ordered two lattes and a plain milk. In a bowl.

I shrugged. I guess I really didn't expect a pig to drink from a cup after all.

She came back in a couple minutes to pick up the coffee.

"I have to go to work," she said. "We can talk later?"

She went back out the door without waiting for an answer. Typical Karen.

CHAPTER 17

Somehow I made it through the day, closed Lighthouse an hour early, and relieved Jake at Southern Treasures. By the time I locked the front door and turned the sign to "Closed," I was ready for a cool shower and a hot meal, not necessarily in that order.

But whatever I did would have to wait a little longer. Bluebeard needed my attention and he hadn't been getting much of it since the construction project started.

I laughed harshly to myself. Destruction project was more like it; so far all that had happened was that my tidy home now looked like the bombed-out aftermath of a tank battle. Or what I imagined the aftermath of a tank battle would look like.

Which was what I needed to talk to Bluebeard about.

"Upstairs is kind of a wreck," I said as I cleaned his dish and gave him fresh water. I moved slowly, keeping my movements carefully casual, as though that would disguise my trepidation.

Bluebeard fixed one beady eye on me and waited.

"I was thinking," I continued while putting grapes and a few cubes of watermelon in his food dish, "that maybe we ought to find a place to stay while the construction crew is working."

The squawk of anger and outrage was far out of proportion with what I'd expected. I knew he might not agree with moving, might want to argue, or even refuse. But this was another level of distress.

He sounded terrified.

The feathers around his neck fanned out, and with an ear-splitting cry he hurled himself out of the cage toward the high ceiling.

There wasn't room for him to really fly around the shop, but he tried. He caromed off a hanging fluorescent light fixture making it swing wildly.

He landed on a sprinkler pipe and continued screaming down at me, as out-of-control as I had ever seen him.

"So," I muttered, "that went well."

I had no idea why he was so upset, nor what I should do about it. I decided to wait him out, wait for him to come down—both literally and figuratively—and try to get an answer for his behavior.

If he would talk to me.

I was still waiting when Jake appeared at the front door half an hour later. Bluebeard had stopped screaming, but he hadn't made any move to leave his perch on the sprinkler pipe.

I unlocked the door and slipped out onto the sidewalk, letting the door close softly behind me.

"Bluebeard just threw an absolute hissy fit when I brought up the subject of staying somewhere else during the construction," I explained. "I don't know why he's so upset, but he seemed genuinely frightened at the prospect. He's still sitting up on the sprinklers, and I don't know when he'll come down."

"Do you want me to talk to him?"

I shook my head. "I doubt there's anything either of us can do. He just needs time to calm down, usually. Though this isn't like anything I've seen him do before."

"Should I leave you alone? Or would it help if I came back inside with you?"

Traffic poured past us on the highway that formed Keyhole Bay's main drag. Tourist season meant a river of cars through town from early morning until late at night, a steady stream of college kids blowing off steam, families stuffed into minivans, and retirees in big sedans or tiny compacts.

It was the economic lifeblood of our small town, and it pulsed through the streets with the rhythm of the stoplights.

I watched the evening traffic flow past the now-closed stores of our tiny downtown, headed for the cluster of restaurants and motels at either end of the business district. Occasionally a car would swing into the curb in front of the neon "Open" sign of The Grog Shop.

"I'm not sure what would be better," I said. "He's been upset before, sure. He's torn the place up, he's been angry, but he's never acted like he was afraid."

Jake put his arm around me and hugged me in against him. "We can just wait a little longer," he said.

We stood quietly, lost in our own thoughts, but I couldn't stay still for very long. I had to see how Bluebeard was doing.

"Let's go in," I said after a few minutes. "I have to see how he's doing."

Bluebeard had come down from the overhead pipes, but his feathers were still ruffled and he squawked when we opened the door. "No," he shrilled.

"It's okay, Bluebeard." I spoke in a soft tone as I moved closer to him. "No one will make you go anywhere."

As I spoke it occurred to me that there was no way I was going to try to force an angry parrot to do anything he didn't want to. I'd seen what that beak and those claws could do to a hard nutshell. I didn't want to see what they could do to me if he panicked.

He eyed me warily, but he let me approach. I reached a tentative hand his direction and he butted his head against my open palm. I could feel him trembling as he leaned into me.

Clearly there was no way I could take him out of the store.

Jake slid a couple steps closer. He moved slowly, hesitating with each step as I calmed Bluebeard.

Bluebeard's trembling subsided, leaving him withdrawn and exhausted as it always did after an outburst. He burrowed his head into his chest and huddled under my chin.

"You okay, buddy?" Jake spoke softly over my shoulder.

Bluebeard shuddered and relaxed slightly, resting more weight against me. I could feel the tension drain as slow seconds ticked past.

At last he pulled away from me and slid into his cage, signaling that he was ready to withdraw and rest. It was a pattern I recognized and it reassured me that he was recovering from the initial terror.

With Jake's help I went through my routine to shut down the store and settle Bluebeard for the night, covering his cage with a blanket to block the light from outside.

I put my face near the door of the cage and whispered, "You better?"

He fixed one beady eye on me and stared for a moment.

"Trying to &^^&%&$#@** sleep here!"

Yeah, he was feeling better. But Jake and I needed to talk.

On the drive to Jake's I debated how to approach the subject. I couldn't move Bluebeard; that much was obvious. But I wasn't sure I could actually move without him, even for a few weeks. Could I leave him alone every night? And what kind of mischief might he get into if I did?

CHAPTER 18

*L*ost in thought, I didn't notice that Jake wasn't driving home until we were several blocks past the turnoff to his house.

Jake glanced over at me and chuckled softly at my puzzled expression. "I'm hungry," he said, "and I'm guessing you are, too. Curly's okay?"

I grinned and nodded vigorously. The drive-thru might be busy but the service was quick and the burgers were worth the wait. I'd had burgers several times in the last few days, but this was kind of an emergency. Proper nutrition could want another day.

"Thanks," I replied. "Not cooking sounds like an excellent idea for tonight."

Jake kept quiet as we sat in the drive-thru waiting for our burgers, giving me time to think. He seemed to know something important was on my mind, but he didn't push me to talk.

The smell of grilled burger and piping hot fries filled the car when the kid at the window passed over the brown paper bag in exchange for Jake's debit card. My stomach growled loudly, and I grabbed a couple fries while Jake put his card away.

We drove the rest of the way to Jake's in silence, except for the chittering of the ice in our drinks as we cornered. I was glad for the respite as we settled on the patio with our burgers and fries, even though I knew we would have to talk at some point.

I ate slowly, as though I could somehow delay the inevitable, but Jake wolfed his burger, then disappeared back into the house.

He emerged a couple minutes later with a small bowl of unshelled peanuts that he set on the small picnic table in front of me.

I looked up, questioning.

"For the elephant," he said. "If he's going to keep hanging around the room, I might as well feed him." His tone was light but I could see the concern in his gaze. He didn't push, but he let me know he was concerned.

With a sigh I set the remnants of my burger on the table next to the half-eaten order of fries. The food was as delicious as always, but my ravenous appetite had disappeared and I didn't expect it to come back.

Maybe ever.

"You don't have to decide anything right now," Jake said. "But it might help to talk it out."

I sighed and hung my head. Was this a conversation I could have with him? Was this the time and place, or could I stall a little longer?

"I'm not going anywhere," Jake said, planting a light kiss on the top of my head. "I'll be here when you're ready."

I looked up. He caught my gaze and held it steady. "When you're ready," he repeated.

I had been on my own since I was a teenager and I had no context, no experience that told me how to handle my churning emotions.

I was never going to be ready, so I told myself it didn't really matter. Now was as good a time as any.

"I'm..." I stopped, chewing on my lower lip. "I'm..." I was stammering was what I was. "I don't know what I am." It felt as whiny as it sounded, and I reacted with disgust at the weakness I displayed.

I stood up abruptly and paced across the patio, first one way and then the other. I don't know if I thought better on my feet, but I sure felt better moving around rather than sitting still, and standing up put me on a level with Jake instead of peering up at him.

He let me make a couple laps, then stepped into my path.

I stopped, took a deep breath, and swallowed hard.

Ready or not, I had to deal.

"I'm scared," I said. "And angry, and sad, and worried, and uncertain. I'm confused, and a little lost. And mostly I don't know how the hell I really feel.

"I don't know what the rules are," I blurted.

Rules for what? I wondered. Rules for my relationship with Jake? Rules for Bluebeard? Rules for Uncle Louis? Rules for how I was supposed to live my life?

Rules for murder? The murders that kept dropping into my life?

"What rules?" Jake asked, as though he was inside my head. He kept the distance between us but his posture invited me closer, the way you let a skittish animal approach you instead of invading their space.

"Any rules!"

"Do you have to have rules?" he asked, furrowing his brow.

"Of course," I answered without thinking. "There are rules for everything, it's what keeps life from spinning out of control. And right now I am pretty close to complete chaos."

Jake grinned at me. "Chaos might do you some good," he said. "Shake things up a bit."

A flash of anger shot through me. "My life is pretty shook up already, in case you haven't noticed. My house looks like the aftermath of a tank battle, Shiloh is dragging Chloe into this Fowler mess, and Chloe and Bluebeard are dragging me along, somebody tried to bring a pig into the coffee shop this morning, and Bluebeard has lost his damned mind.

"I think that's plenty of chaos for one person."

"Well, Bluebeard—" He stopped short. "A pig? Really? They tried to bring in a pig? On a leash, or—"

"In a stroller!" I shouted. "At first I thought it was the ugliest kid I had ever seen, but—"

Jake's roar of laughter stopped me short. How dare he laugh at what I was going through? It wasn't funny.

Well, okay. The pig thing was a little funny.

In fact, it was very funny.

A giggle broke through the wall of anger and misery I had built around myself, and invited its friends to join the party. Soon I was in Jake's arms, leaning against his solid chest, laughing until tears rolled down my face and I couldn't catch my breath.

"Yes," I gasped between bouts of uncontrollable laughter, "a little pink pig."

More laughter.

"In a freakin' stroller!"

Jake held me until I finally regained control, then led me inside to the sofa and gently pushed me into it. I didn't resist. I was too weak to even argue.

He sat next to me, giving me a moment to collect myself before he spoke again.

"Feel better?"

I felt a giggle threatening to break loose and tamped it down. I had to admit it had felt good to just let go, to let the waves of laughter take over and wash away my control, even if only for a minute or two.

I nodded, not trusting myself to speak.

"Now let me tell you what the rules are, if only just for tonight," Jake said, his voice low and thick with emotion.

"Number one, you are not going to give in to fear.

"Number two, we can talk out one worry tonight, and put the rest aside for tomorrow, or the next day, or next week.

"Number three, you do not have to make any decisions or do anything tonight except talk.

"And number four, you will accept the help and support of the man who loves you."

CHAPTER 19

J had never fainted in my life and I wasn't about to start now, but for a moment I think I came close.

My vision narrowed until all I could see was Jake's eyes, dark blue like the deep end of a swimming pool. His voice seemed to come from far away as he asked, "Can you do that?"

I couldn't get enough air into my lungs to answer him and resorted to a mute nod.

Had he actually said he loved me? Did I even hear him right, or was my mind playing tricks on me?

I struggled to breathe as my heart raced. The moment of dizziness passed and I drew a deep breath that caught for a split second before it filled my lungs. The darkness at the edges of my vision receded and the room slowly came back into focus.

"So," he asked, "which worry do you want to tackle?"

I hesitated. I could ask him what he meant by rule number four, but his quick retreat to his earlier rule left me wondering if I really wanted to know the answer.

He could be referring to any number of the men in my life. Guy, who was like an adored uncle; or Riley, the brother I never had; Felipe and Ernie, who defined relationship goals for me; Sly, my link to the generations of family I never knew. They were the family of my heart, and we loved each other more than many families joined by blood.

I struggled to admit to myself that I hoped he had meant something else. Someone else.

I couldn't bear the thought of that hope being dashed. Instead I took the coward's way out and answered his question instead of asking one of my own.

"Bluebeard. I have to figure out what to do with him."

Jake nodded. Clearly he meant for me to talk this out. He wasn't going to offer any quick answers.

"I can't move him. That much is clear."

I stopped and he nodded again. Still not giving me answers.

"The truth is," I said, measuring my words carefully, "I don't know how his world works. Maybe Uncle Louis can't leave the shop; maybe something bad will happen to him."

"Have you taken him out before?" Jake asked. "The vet maybe?"

I had to stop and think about that. Dr. Herman lived just a couple blocks away, and he had been a regular at Lighthouse for as long as I could remember.

Usually he'd drop in at Southern Treasures on his way to work when Bluebeard was due for a checkup or needed a shot. Said it was easier on both of them that way, though maybe he just didn't want the parrot's foul mouth to upset his other clients.

"I wanted to take him for a ride in the truck after Sly sold it to me," I said, my voice adding air quotes around the word sold. We both knew I hadn't paid anywhere near what the vintage pickup was worth.

"I almost took him with me on my very first ride. But after how badly that ended," I shuddered a little, remembering my involuntary visit to the fish tank at the Grotto, "I think I was a little spooked.

"No," I shook my head slowly. "I don't think I've taken him out of the building. At least not since I found out about Uncle Louis."

"Has he ever tried to leave on his own?"

"Um," I stalled, once again searching my memory. "No. When he gets agitated he always goes high, onto the sprinkler pipes, like he wants to be out of reach. Never toward the door, even if it's open."

I shrugged. "I can't be sure of the reason, but it's clear Bluebeard does not want to leave the shop. Whether the bird himself is afraid of the outside world or there's some reason Uncle Louis can't or won't leave, it doesn't really matter. We just have to work around it."

"And we will," Jake assured me. "Just tell me what you want to do."

His deference to my wishes was wearing a little thin. He'd made his point.

"If *we* are going to solve this, I need to know what you think, too. It's not just my choice that matters."

"Your shop. Your bird. Your house. Yes, I think it is your choice that matters."

A flash of anger propelled me to my feet. Just how ridiculous could he be?

I glared down at Jake. "Are you kidding me? If we," I gestured from myself to him and back again, "are going to figure this out, I need to hear what you have to say."

He started to rise, but I pushed him back into his chair. My adrenaline was pumping. Ready or not, I was going to get an answer to the question I had been afraid to ask.

"Did you just say you love me?" I blurted out before I could have second thoughts.

He blinked a couple times as though he hadn't heard me.

"Well, did you?"

"Yeah. Of course. It's not like it's a surprise is it?"

I just stared, dumbfounded. How could any man be that dense?

I didn't have a lot of experience—honestly, I didn't have *any* experience with serious romantic relationships—but I expected declarations of love to come in more romantic ways than this.

I mean, according to Karen she and Riley had done it across a tiny cocktail table at our junior prom, complete with flutes of sparkling apple cider. You'd think I'd at least get a glass of sweet tea, not a list of rules.

I wasn't quite sure how to answer him. I had hoped, sure. Maybe even fantasized a little about how he would finally say it, if he ever did.

Surprised didn't begin to describe how I felt.

More importantly: Did I feel the same way?

It wasn't even a question. I knew I did. But Jake didn't get off quite that easily.

"Well, a little, yeah." I waved my arms in frustration, unable to find the words to explain.

Jake took advantage of my confusion to stand up and take me in his arms. He kissed me, then pulled back and looked in my eyes. "I love you, Glory. Have for a long time."

He pulled me close again. "That better?"

A chuckle escaped, muffled against his chest. I raised my head and looked up at him. "I love you, too."

A look of relief passed over his face, as though he had been unsure of my response.

With one emotional hurdle cleared, I squared my shoulders, took a deep breath, and gestured to the sofa. "Shall we sit back down and try to find an answer to *our* current dilemma?"

CHAPTER 20

*W*e talked late into the night, the conversation slipping from one topic to another, all of them centering on the question of us and our future.

In the end we agreed that Bluebeard would have to remain in the shop, no matter where I might be. It was clear that he couldn't, or wouldn't, be moved and there was no reason to add to his distress.

There were many more decisions to come, and I didn't have all the answers, but I fell asleep in the wee hours of the morning secure in the conviction that I didn't have to face them alone. Jake would be a permanent part of my life.

However, what seemed perfectly reasonable and safe in the soft darkness of night wasn't nearly as comforting in the cold light of early morning.

Despite getting to sleep very late, years of habit had my eyes open at daylight. For an instant I felt safe and content lying next to Jake; then I woke up and the immediate problems rushed back.

With a sigh I crawled out of bed and headed for the kitchen. Today was going to require a *lot* of coffee.

Jake stirred as I belted my robe. I leaned down and kissed his cheek. "Five more minutes," he muttered, still half-asleep.

"Take fifteen," I answered. "I'll start coffee and grab a shower."

He didn't argue, instead sighing happily and burrowing back into his pillow.

Half an hour later, showered and with an initial hit of caffeine, we parked the car behind Beach Books. Jake didn't open the store until midmorning, but knowing Chloe would have freshly-baked quiche at Lighthouse gave us an excuse to skip cooking breakfast. Since I lived just upstairs, eating breakfast, and often lunch, at Lighthouse had quickly become a habit after I bought the coffee shop.

Would that have to change if I moved, even for a few weeks? Would Jake be willing to come in early, or skip breakfast? And what about lunch?

Fretting about meals kept my mind away from my biggest worry. As we crossed the still-quiet main drag of Keyhole Bay heading for breakfast, I caught myself staring at the front window of Southern Treasures.

I'd left Bluebeard alone overnight, and I couldn't help wondering what kind of mischief he might have gotten himself into while I was gone.

Was he still distressed? He had seemed better when we left, but what if he woke up in the middle of the night and took it into his head to trash the shop? Or to leave me some cryptic clue to puzzle over?

In any case, I needed to find out before Julie came in.

I unlocked the front door of Lighthouse and quickly locked it behind us, calling out to Chloe that we had come in. A muffled shout from the back acknowledged our presence, and I made out something about quiche.

Leaving Jake to deal with breakfast, I gathered my courage and went next door to check on Bluebeard.

To my surprise and relief, the shop appeared untouched. The only evidence of the irascible parrot was a muttered curse from the back of his cage.

I retrieved a small bowl of grapes from the storeroom and added half a banana and a few nuts. Indulgent, yes, but I wanted to reward his good behavior and I wasn't above bribery. Placing the bowl inside the cage, I whispered that I'd be back and headed for breakfast.

As I reached the connecting door, Bluebeard stuck his head out of the cage and fixed one beady eye on me. "All her fault," he said clearly before retreating.

Jake was waiting with steaming mugs of coffee when I returned to Lighthouse. "Everything okay?" he asked.

"That blasted bird," I began, then stopped when I saw the stricken look on his face. "No, no, not like that," I said hastily. "He didn't tear anything up. He's just playing his stupid pronoun game."

From his expression he clearly didn't understand what I meant. "He never seems to give me an actual *name*. It's always 'him' or 'her' or 'bad man' or 'pretty girl' and I can never be sure exactly who he's talking about."

Chloe appeared from the back with two plates of quiche and fresh fruit. At my invitation, she dashed into the back and grabbed a plate for herself and joined us at the table.

"Ten minutes," she said, pulling up another chair. "I have cinnamon rolls in the oven."

I sniffed, catching the sweet smell coming from the kitchen. "They smell wonderful!"

"They won't if I let them burn."

"How's Shiloh? And Joe?" I asked around a bite of quiche.

Chloe shook her head. "Not good. Joe's mom keeps having hysterics about this woman who claims she was married to Mr. Fowler, and Joe can't seem to calm her down."

She lowered her voice, even though there wasn't anyone else in the shop. "Shiloh says Joe had to call her doctor from down in Pensacola to give her something."

"Pensacola?" Jake asked.

"Oh, Kerrie wouldn't allow anyone from a 'backwater town' to treat her," I said. "She always thought she was too good for this place."

"That's part of why she's so upset," Chloe continued. "She always told Joe that someday she was going to get out of here, with or without her husband.

"And now that she doesn't have to wait for him to agree, she's stuck until this whole will issue is resolved."

A timer chirped in the kitchen and Chloe jumped up, grabbing her empty plate and hurrying back to rescue the cinnamon rolls. "I'll bring more coffee in a minute," she called over her shoulder.

"No need," Jake said, rising to follow her. "I'll get it."

He returned with a carafe and refilled our mugs. "Do you think that might be the 'she' Bluebeard was talking about?"

I shrugged. I didn't want to believe Kerrie was capable of hurting, no killing, Matt Fowler. Still, I couldn't completely dismiss the idea.

"I don't know. She's put up with a lot from him over the years, but she seemed to accept the new cars and jewelry and the occasional cruise as reason enough to stay."

"Maybe she'd had enough," Jake suggested. "Or maybe she found out about this other family. Just because she didn't tell Joe about it doesn't mean she didn't know."

I nodded, conceding his point. "But there's also the other wife. What if she came looking for Fowler and they got into a fight? I mean, if you believe her story, they were divorced and she was left with a child to raise on her own. Who knows how she felt about him after all these years? Especially when he looked like he was doing well."

"Maybe she wanted money and he refused.

"Maybe that's the 'her' Bluebeard was talking about."

It was Jake's turn to shrug. "We don't even know the cause of death. Maybe it was just an accident, and the whole family drama has nothing to do with it."

"Not with Bluebeard raising six kinds of Cain. He's only ever done that when there was a murder involved. It's like Uncle Louis has some connection and he wants me to do something about it.

"I need to call Karen. See if Doc Frazier has released a cause of death. But I still don't think it's an accident."

I thought back to the first time Bluebeard had drawn me into an investigation. When the quarterback of the local football team was killed in a one-car crash on a deserted back road, Bluebeard had said clearly, "It wasn't an accident."

Now another man was dead, ironically the man who had employed both the quarterback and his killer. It looked like an accident and Bluebeard was acting out once again.

No, I didn't think this was an accident.

CHAPTER 21

"*A*ccepting for the moment that the first wife really was married to Fowler, *if*," Jake raised a finger to emphasize the word, "it wasn't an accident—which I am not saying it wasn't—and *if* we take what Bluebeard said to mean that there's a woman involved, that still doesn't mean that it's either of Fowler's wives.

"From everything I've heard about the man, it seems like there should be plenty of women around who aren't exactly in the Matthew Fowler Fan Club."

I nodded. "I've heard rumors about every woman that worked for him." A vague memory tickled the back of my brain. "I heard something," I began, then stopped and shook my head. "Nope. I can't remember who it was, or exactly how his name came up, but somebody mentioned him, and not in a good way."

I knew it was going to bug me until the comment came back to me, but trying to remember wasn't going to make it happen.

I shoved the thought aside. Whatever it was, it would probably come back in the middle of the night.

"But if it isn't one of them," I asked, "then who would it be?"

Jake shook his head. "No idea. You're the one who's lived here forever."

"All I have is rumors. And Bluebeard."

I glanced at the clock as Chloe breezed back through to unlock the front door and turn over the "Open" sign. With a sigh I gathered up my dishes and headed for the kitchen. "Time for me to get moving. Maybe I'll think of something else later."

But I didn't. Construction noise distracted me throughout the morning and well into the afternoon. With customers, ordering, phone calls, Bluebeard, and all the usual commotion of summer in a tourist town, it was closing time before I realized, and I still hadn't had time to get back to the newspapers Bluebeard had left out.

I still hadn't heard from Karen by the time I locked the front door so I gave her a call. When she answered I could hear the background hum of traffic and the slight echo that told me she was on the speaker in her car.

"They're still talking as if it was an accident," she told me when I asked about the investigation. "And really, if the feds and the locals are willing to go along with that, do we have any reason to think it isn't?"

"Bluebeard." I said it without hesitation. "He has never gotten this worked up unless there was a murder involved, and this is the worst I have ever seen."

I told her about his outburst the night before, and his insistence that a woman was at fault. "But he doesn't give me a name, just 'her fault,' and 'woman trouble.'"

I sighed impatiently. "I wish I could be sure what he means. Or that he'd at least give me a clue."

"But he's not going to, and you know that," she replied. "So for now we just have to wait until Boomer and Dr. Frazier release the autopsy results."

"I suppose," I said, reluctantly. "Unless..."

"Unless what?" Karen's voice was wary. "You aren't thinking what I think you're thinking. Are you?"

I tried to sound innocent, but I've never been a very good liar. "I have no idea what you mean."

"Gloryanna Martine," she answered in her best stern-mom voice, "you know exactly what I am talking about.

"You are hatching some scheme to involve yourself in a police investigation, maybe get yourself arrested for interfering with the police, maybe even tangle with the Feds, and generally put yourself in harm's way. All on the word of a stressed-out parrot."

"Or my uncle," I shot back, but I knew she was right.

"So," Karen went on, ignoring my response, "what are we going to do?"

"We?"

"If you think for one minute you are going to go digging into this without me, you are sorely mistaken. Sorely mistaken," she repeated, just in case I hadn't heard her the first time.

"I don't know where to start. I want to get a look at that repair bay, just to refresh my memory."

I hurried on before she could object. "I probably should go back over the newspapers Bluebeard left out, and maybe dig around Fowler's history, see what else we can find."

"Now you're getting into my expertise," she said, ignoring my idea of prowling around Fowler's repair shop.

"Why don't you bring the papers over here," the phone cut off from the speaker as she shut off the engine, signaling her arrival at home. "We can order another pizza and I'll see what I can dig up on Fowler and the story of another family."

"Jake—" I started, but she cut me off.

"Bring him along. The more eyes on this stuff the better." I heard her fumble with her key ring as she unlocked the front door. "Besides, Riley should be home soon so it will be the four of us." She took a quick segue off-ramp.

"I better call him to pick up the pizza on the way."

I tried to argue, but the phone was already dead in my hand. I thought about calling her back, but I knew she'd be calling Neil's to order pizza or calling Riley to order him to pick it up.

Karen was good at orders.

Truth was, I should have known what would happen from the instant I decided to call. When Karen Freed got an idea in her head there was no room for argument. I'd known that since second grade, so what made me think I could change her now?

Instead I dialed Beach Books and filled Jake in on our plans. "If that works for you," I added.

Jake laughed. "It's fine. Besides, do you really think you're going to get her to change her plans once she's made them?"

He had apparently read my mind.

Twenty minutes later, with Bluebeard settled for the night and a stack of vintage newspapers carefully laid out in back seat, we pulled up in front of Karen and Riley's house.

The pizza was still steaming when Riley opened the box on Karen's prized chrome-and-Formica table.

I carefully placed the newspapers on the cocktail table in the living room. If Bluebeard had managed not to damage the fragile newsprint, they should be protected from pizza-stained fingers.

Time enough to look at them after we ate.

If I could wait that long.

CHAPTER 22

$\mathcal{T}$he aroma of tomato sauce, pepperoni, and wood-fired crust filled the kitchen as Riley pried the tops off long-necked bottles of beer and passed them around.

We quickly dug in, cheese trailing off the steaming pieces as we pulled them from the box. Conversation came to a near standstill, the silence punctuated by the occasional yelp as molten cheese hit a lip or tongue.

I wasn't the only one who was anxious to get to the papers though. Karen wolfed down a single slice before hastily washing her hands and grabbing her beer.

"I want to see what Bluebeard thinks is so important," she said, heading for the living room. "The rest of you can catch up when you're done."

I popped the last bite of my slice into my mouth and followed her example. "I'll show you what we have so far," I mumbled around a mouthful of pepperoni and cheese. "Just give me a sec."

I saw Riley and Jake exchange a look before they each grabbed another slice. "Right behind you," Riley said before he took a huge bite.

Jake nodded in agreement, his mouth already full.

By the time the two men had joined us in the living room, Karen and I had arranged the newspapers in chronological order and I was pointing out the articles Jake and I had already read.

"This was the newest one." I pointed to the birth announcement. "October, 1989. And this," I patted the front pages of the society page with the elegant portrait of a young Kerrie McKenzie, "is from that April.

"You'll notice there's only about six months in between."

"Oops." Karen chuckled. "But it's not like they were the first. Or the last."

"No," I agreed nodding. "But from what I have heard, Fowler was cutting a pretty wide swath through the single, and maybe not-so-single, women of Keyhole Bay.

"Getting married might have cramped his style a bit."

"Not from what I heard," she said.

I shot her a look and suddenly remembered where I'd heard a reference to Matt Fowler.

Karen's mother. She had worked for Fowler briefly, very briefly, after her divorce from Karen's dad, the Miller in Catherine Miller Evans Pearson Fontaine. Now settled down with Clint Fontaine, AKA Stepdad Number Three, she had made a passing reference to Fowler when she was in town for Karen and Riley's wedding. It wasn't anything specific, but she certainly wasn't a member of the Matthew Fowler Fan Club.

Not many women were.

I filed the recollection for later and turned back to the newspapers, looking for the next date.

Riley held the paper, his hand poised to turn the page. Jake touched his arm, stopping him midmotion. "Bluebeard left them open to specific pages," he explained. "So there's something on this particular page he wants us to see."

Riley stopped and spread the paper across the table where we could all examine the open page. It took a minute, then Jake spotted the small announcement on the far righthand side, almost to the fold.

"Fowler Automotive Opens Dealership" read the bold-faced headline. Three short paragraphs followed, giving the location and hours of the new business and closing with a quote from the proud young owner. "This dealership is just the first step in our plan to serve the automotive needs of the entire region."

"Not that he's bragging or anything," Karen said.

I started to chuckle, then stopped myself. Fowler had been an ego on two legs certainly, but the man was dead and I was convinced he'd been murdered. There was nothing funny about any of this.

Jake shook his head. "Those 'new business' stories are pretty stock," he said. "I know when they ran one on me taking over Beach Books I think I gave them about 3 sentences. They turned it into three paragraphs and I'll bet it sounded pretty similar."

Karen cocked an eyebrow at him. "You planning to take over the book needs of the entire region, are you?"

Jake shook his head. "Not yet," he joked.

One newspaper remained on the table, open to the sports page. I was again reminded that my involvement with crime-solving in Keyhole Bay had started with the death of the high school's star quarterback. Bluebeard seemed to be bringing me full circle.

Riley spotted the item this time. "Local football star reveals his college choice," he read. "Star quarterback Matthew Fowler announced this week that he has accepted a football scholarship from Florida State University and has signed a letter of intent."

"What's the date on that one?" Jake asked.

"February 12, 1986," Riley read from the top of the page.

"And when did he open the dealership?" Jake reached for the previous paper, glancing at the date. "September of 1987. That's only a year and a half.

"It looks like Mr. Fowler didn't spend long in Tallahassee."

"A year at the most," Riley said. "He would have started in September of '86 and he was back in Keyhole Bay and opening a car lot a year later."

"Where did the money come from?" Karen wondered aloud. "I don't recall his parents having the kind of money to bankroll a car dealership."

We all exchanged glances, and Karen jumped up from the sofa. "I'll get the laptop."

I watched in awe as Karen's fingers flew across the keyboard. I understood that she was searching for information about Matthew Fowler, and that anyone could search the internet. But it still looked like magic to me.

It wasn't just searching, it was knowing *where* to search. Karen seemed to know every public archive, every private database, and every convoluted route to obscure information. I was pretty sure she had off-line resources too, everywhere in Florida, and probably beyond.

But Matthew Fowler proved a challenge, even for Karen's magic. She spent several minutes confidently tapping away, her frustration visibly mounting and her confidence waning as she ran up against one block after another.

Soon she sounded like she was taking vocabulary lessons from Bluebeard.

"Not a lot in the usual places," she said with a note of disgust. "Not like he was hiding his history, there are plenty of local news stories about his company, and lots of puff pieces about his involvement in the community."

"Which conveniently mention the dealership?" Sarcasm dripped from Riley's every word.

Karen shrugged. "Face it, we all know Fowler didn't have an altruistic bone in his body.

"The real surprise is that so far I haven't found any real scandals tied to him. Those he *did* manage to hide."

"He must have," I said. "Because we all know they were there."

Jake gave me a quizzical look, and I was reminded he'd only been in town a few years.

"He had a reputation, like we said. Thought of himself as a real ladies' man. Even though he married fairly young, there were always rumors of him being involved with one woman or another—some single, some not."

"I remember something," Riley said slowly. "Way back, when I was working as a deckhand on *Wave Rider*. Ricky—you remember Ricky, moved to the West Coast about ten years ago?"

He scowled as he tried to remember decade-old gossip. "Anyway, Ricky and his wife were having some problems. Came pretty close to divorce, as I recall. We came back early from a trip, and word was Ricky caught his wife," he paused, searching his memory for her name.

"Claudia." Karen lifted her head from the screen long enough to provide the missing information, then went back to searching and muttering.

"That's it! Ricky supposedly caught Claudia with Fowler. A couple of the guys said there was a real knock-down, drag-out, someone called the cops, and Ricky was tossed in jail to cool down."

"That I might be able to find," Karen said. She typed faster, a grim smile of determination on her face.

"So how did Fowler keep that quiet?" Jake asked.

Riley grinned. "The next week Kerrie was driving a brand-new Cadillac," he answered. "Claudia bailed Ricky out of jail, though nobody really knew where she got the cash.

"Hell, money was one of the things they were always fighting about. A couple weeks later he got an offer for the boat. Good price, all cash, a chance to start over somewhere away from Keyhole Bay."

He shrugged. "Last I heard was a few years back. They patched things up and found a place on the coast up in Washington."

"Aha!" Karen's shout made me jump, and we all turned to look at her.

"Ricky Johnson was a guest of the city for one night in July of '06. Simple assault," she tapped a few more keys. "Pled to a misdemeanor, credit for time served. That's all from the newspaper's archives. Might be more in the court records, but I doubt it; they pretty much print the police log and the court records verbatim."

"Whatever happened to *Wave Rider*?" I asked Riley. "I don't recall seeing that name on any of the current fleet."

Riley furrowed his brow, then smiled. "She got renamed. Old man Noble bought her from Ricky and now she's the *Eastwind*."

"Hadn't thought about that in a long time." His grin spread a little wider. "I think that was the first time I had spiced rum."

"What?" Jake asked.

"Renaming ceremony," Riley answered. "It's considered bad luck to rename a boat, but Noble figured the boat was already bad luck, considering. So we had a ceremony, burned the old log books, scrubbed the name from the hull, and rechristened her.

"A shot for the ocean, a shot for the boat, and then a shot for everyone aboard. I was strictly a beer guy, but Noble said if she was gonna sail the Gulf, we should drink rum."

He shook his head. "Still not a fan."

"I'll keep that in mind," Jake deadpanned.

CHAPTER 23

Karen had continued her tapping while Riley told his story. "Well!" she exclaimed before Riley could respond. "I think we have something here."

I scooted over closer to look at the open laptop, and both Riley and Jake came to lean over the back of the sofa to see what she had found.

I scanned the screen full of tiny print, but I couldn't figure out exactly what Karen was looking at.

Impatient, I glared at her. "Would you like to share with the rest of the class, Miss Smarty-Pants?"

"Sorry," she replied, though she didn't sound very sorry. "I went looking for records in Leon County between September 1986 and June 1987, when Fowler was in Tallahassee. Kind of a long shot, but I think I've struck paydirt."

She pointed at a line in the middle of the page. "Matthew Fowler and Louisa Melissa Frances Pope filed for the annulment of their marriage on May 14, 1987."

"Annulment?" Riley said. "I thought that meant the marriage never happened. How is a marriage that didn't happen even part of the public record?"

Karen fidgeted, opening another browser window and typing in "Louisa Pope."

"It kind of isn't..." she muttered.

"Karen." Riley's voice held a note of warning.

"It's okay, Riley. The *annulment* isn't in the vital statistics like a marriage or divorce, but the *petition* and the order are part of the court records. You just have to dig a little deeper."

The whole time she was explaining her fingers were flying over the keyboard. A few seconds later the image of a young woman with long blonde hair and the megawatt smile of a beauty queen filled the screen.

"Louisa Pope, ladies and gentlemen. Miss Leon County, 1986."

We all stared at the woman, as though just seeing her picture would somehow give us some insight into the woman who had been, however briefly, Matthew Fowler's first wife.

"He always was one for pretty girls," Karen commented as she opened yet another search.

Behind me I felt Jake shrug. "Was always partial to brunettes myself," he said, squeezing my shoulder. The gesture made me smile.

"And here are her parents. Leland and Marjorie Pope. Pillars of the community." She scanned quickly, the page scrolling by faster than I could read. "Looks like Leland passed away this spring. Hmmm," she continued reading. "Marjorie moved to West Palm, turning over the family business," she paused dramatically, then continued in her best announcer's voice, "an automotive sales empire, to her only child, Louisa Pope Cleveland and her family."

We all exchanged glances. "I don't believe in coincidence," Riley said at last. "So how did their former son-in-law, their only child's spouse for about a nanosecond, establish his own little automotive empire just a few months after his marriage to that child was annulled?

"Does anyone in this room believe for a second that these two things aren't connected?

"Anyone?"

Karen stopped her tapping and looked around at her husband.

"You know how I feel. The real question is what are we going to do about it?"

"Time for a road trip?" I said lightly. "Maybe drop in on the previous Mrs. Fowler?"

Jake's hand tightened on my shoulder. "Seems like Karen is getting plenty of information from right here."

"Besides," Karen said, turning a stern gaze my direction, "you already have a lot to do here with construction and all.

"And, as you've reminded me so often, 'dropping in' without an invitation is something reserved for family and your closest friends. Certainly not for someone you've never met."

I leaned back, startled. Who was this person advising caution and good manners? Certainly not the Karen who had joined me on several unannounced visits. Including a couple that involved locked doors.

Outnumbered, I decided to make a strategic retreat. I'd give Karen the benefit of the doubt and get to the bottom of her uncharacteristic caution later. Preferably without an audience.

"So what else do we know about the beauty queen?" I asked. "I assume Cleveland is a married name, and the thing about her dad mentioned a family. So I'd guess there is—or was—another husband. And children."

Karen turned back to her laptop. A search for Louisa Cleveland immediately turned up a current husband who owned an insurance agency, and three kids.

Anson Cleveland, her oldest, was born in late January, 1988.

I stared at the dates for a few seconds, my brain doing some quick calculations.

"Anson Cleveland was born less than eight months after the marriage was annulled." I said softly.

"He's Matthew Fowler's son."

"We can't be sure of that," Jake said. "What if she was already involved with Cleveland when she married Fowler, and that's why the annulment? Or maybe he really was a little early?"

"Look up the husband," Riley told Karen. "See what it says about him."

James Cleveland ran for city council in a suburb of Tallahassee a few months earlier. His campaign bio prominently featured his photo in a Navy officer's uniform. According to the accompanying service dates, he was in the Persian Gulf the first half of 1987. He couldn't have been Anson's father.

"So much for that theory," Riley shrugged.

Karen closed the laptop and set it on the coffee table with an impatient grunt. "Enough.

"We know Bluebeard is giving us some kind of crazy clues, and that Fowler's first wife showed up and threw Kerrie into a real hissy fit, but that's really all we know.

"The rest of this," she gestured at the closed laptop, "is just guessing."

"Maybe so," I said. "But I'll still take Bluebeard's word over anything else.

"No matter what Boomer says, I am not going to believe this was an accident."

CHAPTER 24

*W*hen Jake and I started home we weren't any closer to a solution to the death of Matthew Fowler. I knew it was a job for the police, and that Boomer would be mightily unhappy if he caught me interfering.

We aren't interfering, we're following up on Bluebeard's clues. Besides, Boomer would laugh me out of his office the minute I told him where the information came from. And since he wouldn't take it seriously, I had to, didn't I?

Yeah, Boomer wouldn't buy that explanation, but it was all I had, and I intended to hold on to it.

"So," Jake said slowly, "are we going back to your place? I figured we'd stay at my place after dinner on Thursday, so you might want to be home for a night or two."

I nodded. "Yes," I answered. "You're welcome to stay, but I'm sure you'll be more comfortable in a place that isn't complete chaos."

Jake chuckled. "Stop apologizing for your construction. It doesn't bother me." He took one hand off the steering wheel and patted my knee. "Just keep imagining how great it will be when it's done. In the meantime, I think I can handle a little chaos, and Bluebeard will be happy to have you home."

"I just want my kitchen back," I grumbled. "I like pizza and burgers just fine, but not as a steady diet. And with the town full of tourists, every restaurant is packed.

"Why did I even think I could do this during the summer?"

"Maybe because the crew was available?" Jake said as he pulled up behind Southern Treasures.

That much was true. When I started looking for construction bids, even getting someone to come out and look at the job had taken weeks, and the actual work had to be booked months in advance. I was at the mercy of Tim's schedule, and I knew it.

For once Bluebeard didn't yell at me when we came in. It wasn't until I got to the top of the stairs that I realized I'd gone directly to Karen's after work and hadn't checked on the progress upstairs.

I hesitated with my hand on the doorknob. Jake nearly ran into me.

"Something wrong?" he asked, concern evident in his voice.

I shook my head, reined in my imagination, and opened the door. The apartment was pitch dark and I fumbled for the light switch, cringing in anticipation of the disaster awaiting me.

To my surprise it wasn't noticeably worse than when I'd last seen it. Or maybe I was just numbed to how awful the mess had become. The room that had once been my living room and kitchen was empty, the walls bare. A stack of cabinets against the front wall looked shabby and forlorn, and a heavy orange extension cord snaked around the wall into the darkness above Lighthouse providing a clue as to the location of the refrigerator.

As for the sink, not only was it missing, but the only evidence that it had ever been there was a couple pipes sticking out of the wall, with newly-installed caps covering the ends.

Actually, it looked a little better than the last time I'd been up here and my hopes rose. Maybe it wouldn't be a disaster after all. Maybe Jake was right; I just had to think about how great it would be when it was finished.

I was still feeling a glimmer of hope the next morning as Jake and I shared quiche and coffee at what was quickly becoming "our" table in the back corner of Lighthouse.

I sighed as I pushed away my empty plate. "I could get used to this," I said. "Having someone make me coffee and cook my breakfast every morning."

"Me too," Jake said. "Especially when I don't have to drive all the way across town."

It was a running joke among the locals, one Jake had picked up on. When you lived in a small town, especially one that filled with tourist traffic several months out of the year, the five or six miles from one end of town to the other quickly became a significant distance.

"It is kind of luxurious having this just downstairs," I agreed. But Jake's expression hinted at more than the momentary luxury.

I bit my lip and glanced at the empty tables around us. I knew the shop wasn't open yet, but still I had to be sure.

"Are you getting used to being here?" I asked. "I mean, do you like it here?"

"Here? As in, Keyhole Bay? Or *here* here?" He gestured toward the apartment over our heads.

"Here," I answered, shooting a glance overhead, trying not to show how nervous the question made me.

"Yeah, I am." Jake reached for my hand and held it tightly as he spoke. "I like it *here*, with you. Like having breakfast with you.

"Especially," he said with a lopsided grin as he shot a look over my shoulder, "when it involves excellent quiche."

I turned to follow his gaze and realized Chloe was approaching with the coffee pot. No wonder he was trying to lighten the mood; this wasn't exactly the place for a serious discussion of our future.

When Chloe unlocked the shop a few minutes later, Karen was the first person through the door. She made a beeline for our table, and Chloe appeared within seconds with a cup of coffee.

"Do you want something to eat?" Chloe asked, but before Karen could answer, the door opened and Shiloh Weaver came in, glanced around, and rushed over to embrace Chloe.

Chloe returned the hug. "Are you okay? Shouldn't you be at work?"

"Not for another hour," Shiloh said. She smiled a bit shakily. "Some of us don't start at the crack of dawn."

Jake stood up and offered Shiloh his chair, but she shook her head. "Didn't mean to barge in on your breakfast. Sorry."

She turned to me. "Hi, Miss Glory. How are you doing?"

It was an automatic courtesy, as was the "Miss Glory," but she waited for my equally-automatic "Fine."

The young woman looked as though she hadn't slept in a week, and she practically vibrated with barely-contained stress.

I stood up and pulled over a chair. "Here, sit down. Not barging in at all." I gently pushed the chair against the back of her legs and she collapsed into it.

"Chloe," I instructed, "Get Shiloh some quiche, and a cup of coffee. You can join us too. Just turn the "Open" sign over for an extra fifteen minutes."

Chloe couldn't hide her surprise, and I wished I could claim I was doing this strictly out of consideration for Shiloh, but I knew I had an ulterior motive. We had been looking for more information about Fowler's murder—I refused to think of it as an accident—and here was a source close to the family, dropped into my lap.

I'd feel guilty about that later. For now there was a chance to gain some insight into what was going on.

Chloe didn't give me a chance to change my mind, and within a couple minutes we were all gathered around the small table, dishes crowded together and a pot of coffee nearby.

Shiloh took a tentative nibble of the quiche, as though she had forgotten how to eat, quickly followed by another, larger, bite. My guess was that she hadn't been eating either.

"So?" Chloe said.

Shiloh looked at the circle of faces around the table. She didn't know the rest of us very well, but the need for someone, anyone, to listen to her concerns overrode her caution. I could see her expression shift from wariness to desperation to surrender in a matter of seconds.

"I'm worried about Joe."

"Joe?"

She turned to Jake. "Joe Fowler. My boyfriend."

He nodded. The rest of us knew about Joe and Shiloh, but Jake wasn't quite as well-versed on Keyhole Bay gossip.

"What's wrong?" Chloe gave her friend an encouraging hug. I was sure she could also see that Shiloh needed to talk.

"You know he found his dad, right?" She glanced around the table again and we all nodded. "That shook him up a lot. I think it was pretty ugly, but he won't tell me anything about what he saw.

"But that's not the worst part. He's upset by what he saw, sure. But he doesn't seem all that broken up about his dad.

"It's almost like he's, I don't know, relieved sort of."

An uneasy silence settled over the table. I waited, hoping someone would speak up, but when no one did I finally said softly, "From what I saw, Matthew didn't treat Joe very well. Do you think that might be affecting his reaction?"

"Or he could still be in shock," Chloe added. "It really has only been a few days. And face it, Shiloh, Fowler wasn't a very nice guy. It must have been hard on Joe to be his kid."

"You have no idea."

The vehemence and bitterness of Shiloh's reply caught me off guard.

"Joe knew about the stuff he did. He wouldn't have hurt his dad, but he hated the fact that he was a letch and a cheater."

Shiloh hesitated, then spoke defiantly. "He tried it on with everything in a skirt. Everything."

Karen raised one eyebrow at Shiloh and the younger woman flushed. "Yes," she said. "Even after I started going out with Joe. In fact, he seemed even more determined after I was dating his son.

"Why do you think I finally quit? The man didn't know the meaning of 'No.'"

I made a mental note to remind Karen later that her own mother had said almost the same thing.

"He's madder at his mom, to tell the truth. Says she put up with this for so long it was like she was enabling him, letting him get away with the stuff he pulled.

"Mostly, though, he just won't talk to me about it. Says he doesn't want to dump on me. But I know he's talking to the new guy over at Fowler's."

"New guy?" Chloe asked.

"Yeah. He started a few weeks ago and he and Joe hit it off right away. It wasn't like he was his boss or anything, though I guess that might change now that Mr. Fowler's gone. But Joe's running the service department, and Anson's in sales."

"Anson?" I blurted out.

"Yeah. Anson Cleveland." Shiloh wrinkled her brow at me. "Do you know him?"

"No. Of course not." I tried not to stammer. "Just an unusual name. That's all."

I caught Karen's eye and knew we would have a long talk about "the new guy" at Fowler's dealership.

CHAPTER 25

The front door rattled as early customers arrived in search of caffeine and sugar.

Chloe jumped up from the table. "I better let them in," she said as she hurried across the shop, flipping over the sign and the deadbolt simultaneously.

Shiloh looked around the table once again, coloring with embarrassment at her revelations. "I didn't mean to dump on you guys," she said. "But I can't talk to my family about this. My mother hated Mr. Fowler, and she thinks Joe is just as bad, just because he's his son."

We reassured her it was okay and she left for work, seemingly less agitated than she had been. I hoped so. She was going through a tough time and I wanted to help, even if my motives weren't entirely pure.

The minute we were alone, Karen pounced. "Anson?!" She looked from me to Jake and back. "Remember what we were saying about coincidence?

"This one would defy the laws of probability."

I shrugged. "No argument here. It's got to be the same guy. How could there be two men with that name? But why? Why did he come to Keyhole Bay? And why did he wait all these years, just to show up a few weeks before Fowler gets killed?

"I'd definitely like to talk to young Mr. Cleveland."

Jake gave me a warning look, but I shook my head. "Maybe I ought to go car shopping," I said. "You know, go over and see what Fowler's has on the lot. Get to know the salesmen, see what kind of a deal they might want to make.

"You know, the truck is great and all, but I could use something a little more anonymous sometimes."

Karen's snort told me she didn't buy my story any more than Jake did. "You're not going without me," she said.

"Don't you have to work?" Jake asked.

"Nine and noon broadcasts," she replied. "Then I'm flexible until the five o'clock slot. Unless there's something immediate in-between. But maybe visiting Fowler's would be good background on the ongoing investigation."

She grinned at Jake. "No way I'm letting her go over there alone. And if you go along every salesman in the place will talk to you, not her."

Jake couldn't argue with that one. We'd already had far too many of those uncomfortable moments. It had happened just a few weeks ago; one of the contractors assumed Jake was in charge of making the decisions about my remodel. After our talk the other night I think Jake was anxious to avoid another such moment.

As though to underscore the thought of the remodel, my phone buzzed with a message. Tim and his crew would be here in a quarter hour.

Karen and I made plans to visit the car lot after lunch, and Jake reluctantly agreed not to join us.

"Besides," I said, giving him a quick kiss before he headed over to open Beach Books, "it's not like I'm actually going to buy a car, so I won't need your help."

He tried to grin, but it took an effort. "Just be careful," he said. "Promise me."

"I promise." For once I didn't try to argue that he was being over-protective. The dealership should be a perfectly safe place to talk to

Anson, but we had no idea what kind of man he was or why he was here.

I skipped lunch, telling myself I just wasn't hungry, I'd had a big breakfast. My stomach wasn't jumpy because I was going to question a stranger about the murder of his father.

If he even knew Fowler was his father. But why else would he come to a tiny tourist town like Keyhole Bay?

Karen showed up a few minutes after her noon broadcast. We'd agreed to take her SUV since my truck really was rather conspicuous. She was a beauty, certainly, but there was no way I wanted any salesman to get the idea he could grab her as a trade-in. And I didn't really want to advertise my presence at the crime scene; word was sure to get back to Boomer if I did.

One advantage of being two thirty-something women was that we were largely ignored when we walked onto Fowler's used car lot. The good-ol'-boy power structure of Keyhole Bay still had a strong emphasis on the "boy."

We loitered for several minutes, peering at one generic sedan or hatchback after another, without anyone speaking to us.

Karen glanced around, but no one was approaching. "Did you notice what else Shiloh said?" she said.

"Which thing?" I asked.

"About her parents?"

"That they didn't like Joe because of his father?"

She nodded.

"I noticed. You have to wonder if it's business—heaven knows there are a lot of folks around here who counted their fingers after shaking Matthew Fowler's hand—or something more."

"Yep. Exactly what I thought."

"Your mom," I hesitated, unsure exactly how to ask about her mother's time at Fowler's.

"She only worked here a couple weeks, if I remember it right. I think it was right after Stepdad Number One, and looking back, I realize how desperate she was for money.

"We were so broke, I think if Lucifer himself had offered her a job she would have taken it.

"But she walked out on the job here and washed dishes at Sea Witch. Used to come home every night with leftover chowder and bread, smelling like the deep fryer. On a good night there might be fish or fries if the cooks were feeling generous.

"I was too young to question her choice—I know Fowler paid more than minimum wage—and she never volunteered anything."

I filed that information away. Karen and her mom still didn't have a real close relationship, and I wasn't going to ask her to quiz her mom about Fowler. Not unless we absolutely had to.

CHAPTER 26

*A*bout the time we were ready to give up and start looking for our prey, a young man approached us, looking like he'd drawn the short straw in the go-talk-to-the-womenfolk lottery.

I watched him come close, trying not to stare openly. The resemblance to Fowler wasn't obvious, but there were similarities, if you were looking for them. I was.

He had his father's nose and ears, but the eyes were warm and a bit innocent, a far cry from the predatory gaze of his father. Or maybe we were just too old for him; that had certainly been one of his father's issues.

"Good afternoon, ladies." His voice was a soft drawl, a bit deferential in the manner of well-raised young Southern men. He kept a polite distance, unlike many salesmen who instantly invaded your personal space.

I immediately liked the man, and almost regretted that we were there to try and extract information from him. Almost. I still wanted to know what had happened to Fowler, and I had to remind myself that he could still be a suspect.

"I'm Anson." He stuck out his hand, and Karen took it.

"Karen Freed," she replied with a quick shake, then turned to me. "And this is my friend, Glory Martine.

"She's the one shopping. I'm just here to help."

"Glad to meet you, Glory."

I took the offered hand and shook it. A firm handshake, but not a bone crusher. His hand was warm and dry, and he didn't try to hold that extra second too long.

Was this guy even a salesman?

"I'm kind of new here," he said, turning to look across the crowded lot. "But I know the inventory and I'd love to help you find the right vehicle.

"What are you looking for?"

My brain said *The truth about how your father died,* but my inside voice stayed inside and I said, "Not sure. I have a pickup for company business, but I may be in the market for something smaller for around town."

Anson nodded and surveyed the lot. "We have a couple things," he said. "Depends on how small you want."

He gestured for us to follow him as he moved between vehicles and across the lot. We passed between late-model sedans with signs boasting of their low mileage, monster SUVs touting their horse-power, and minivans claiming to have room for seven passengers. Right, if six of them were under the age of eight—have you ever tried to get in the back row of one of those things?

Anson stopped next to a midsize sedan with giant yellow-card-board letters propped on the windshield spelling SALE.

"Last year's model," he said. "Under warranty, gets 30-plus mpg, all the options—including a moon roof—and because it's not the current year, I think I can get you a sweet deal."

"How does the reliability rate?" Karen said, pulling out her phone as though she had those statistics waiting at her fingertips. In fact I hadn't considered the possibility, but now it seemed likely she did.

Anson looked as though he had hoped we weren't going to ask that question. "There were some factory issues," he admitted. His voice brightened. "But this one has had all the necessary service since it was on the lot here. Shouldn't be any problems going forward."

Taking my cue from Karen, I shook my head slowly. "Maybe not," I said.

Anson, to his credit, didn't try to argue. Instead he moved us along the row to a little red box of a car.

"These have a good reliability rating, and the manufacturer's warranty is one of the best in the business."

He spoke with a confidence that belied his short tenure with Fowler, and it occurred to me that the young man might well know a lot about the auto business, thanks to his grandfather. He might be the low man on this particular totem pole, but it was likely he knew more than most of the salespeople in the dealership.

I wondered if Fowler had recognized that experience when Anson came to work for him.

"You seem to know a lot about cars for someone who's new here," I said with a little laugh.

He nodded, his blond hair catching the afternoon sun, and shrugged. "I worked for my grandfather in Tallahassee before I moved here. He was a tough guy to work for, but I learned a lot."

"Tallahassee?" Karen said. "What an odd coincidence! Mr. Fowler," she bowed her head a fraction of an inch, as though in respect for the deceased, "went to school there. Played football for Florida State until he got injured."

The remark hit home, but as quickly as the reaction appeared it was buried under a bland expression. "Really? I wish I'd known that." He shook his head in a show of sadness. "I didn't get to know him very well. I would have liked to ask him how he liked Tallahassee."

Karen caught my eye, but I wasn't sure what she wanted. She turned away with a pained expression, a look that clearly said *I guess I have to do this myself.*

"How about we take this one for a test ride?" she suggested. "It looks kind of fun. And I love the color!"

Anson quickly excused himself to get the keys, leaving us alone for a minute.

"Why are we taking a test drive?" I whispered. No one had come anywhere near us, but I was still nervous that someone could over-hear our conversation.

Karen rolled her eyes. "Bonding," she said. "Let him think he might have the chance of a sale, and get him away from here. He might talk a little more freely without the rest of the crew around."

Anson returned with the key, cutting our conversation short. He unlocked the car and handed me the key before seating himself in the backseat. Karen instantly jumped into the seat behind me, leaving me to play the part of some insane chauffeur in this charade.

As I adjusted the mirror, I caught sight of Anson's puzzled expres-sion and Karen's serene one. She was in her element now, with her target trapped in a moving vehicle.

I started the engine and pulled out onto the highway.

This was Karen's show now. She was good at reading people and at getting information they didn't want to divulge, so I was content to follow her lead as I drove away from downtown.

"You look like him, you know." Her voice was soft, matter-of-fact.

"What?" Anson was startled, but trying to remain polite.

"Your father," she said. "You do look like him."

"How do you know my father? Have you been to Tallahassee?" He paused as though searching his memory for an answer. "I don't think he's ever been here."

"Not Mr. Cleveland," Karen said in the same conversational tone. "Your biological father."

Anson started to speak, but all I could hear from the back seat was a garbled muttering. Finally he said softly, "I never told you my name was Cleveland."

"No."

"So how do you know so much about me? What are you two up to? Where are you taking me?" His voice rose with an undercurrent of panic. "People know what car we're in! They'll start looking for me if I don't come back right away!"

"Anson!" Karen's voice cut through his panicky babble.

He paused and she jumped into the ensuring silence.

"Glory, let's drive out to Bayvue Estates. We can talk there."

CHAPTER 27

I nodded without looking back. The abandoned housing development still sat on the outskirts of Keyhole Bay. Rumor had it that a contractor from Pensacola was going to revive construction, but for now it was still empty.

We drove in silence for the few minutes it took to reach Bayvue.

I glanced back occasionally—the car had one of those little bubble mirrors for watching the kids in the back seat—to check on Anson. He didn't impress me as the type to jump from a moving vehicle, especially one he was responsible for, but you never know what people will do under stress.

Apparently Karen had the same thought. "We just want to talk," she said gently. "We'll get the car back to the lot in one piece and before anyone thinks we've run off with it."

He didn't look very reassured however, when we pulled into the deserted jumble of partially-paved and rutted dirt streets.

A finished model home sat vacant at the entrance, with several partially-completed houses filling the rest of the block, finally giving way to bare lots that had been graded but not leveled or developed. Scarred and rutted from the storms that had passed through, the lot lines were losing the battle with the encroaching vegetation. Whoever tried to develop this mess was going to have to redo nearly everything the previous owner had done before they went broke.

The pavement ended with a drop-off to gravel, most of it already washed away. In deference to Anson and the car that didn't belong to me, I turned right and pulled around a paved cul-de-sac of empty lots backed by swampland. I stopped about 25 yards from the intersection and shifted to park, but I left the engine running as though to reassure Anson that we didn't intend to stay long.

Karen caught my eye in the mirror, giving me a chance to open the conversation or wait for her.

I didn't wait.

"So, Anson," I asked, keeping my voice low, "why are you here? Why now and not years ago? You're thirty years old. Why not when you turned eighteen? Or twenty-one? Or when you graduated from college?

"Why come at all?"

I turned in my seat to look at him. He was a decade younger than us, but he seemed much younger, more innocent, perhaps more naive. Or maybe the school of hard knocks had simply made me older than my years; but that was a puzzle for another time.

Anson's struggle with the questions was clear on his face. It took him several deep breaths before he was able to speak, seconds that felt like hours to me.

"I wanted to meet him. To see who he really was." He shook his head and laughed, not amused but bitter. "I guess I thought he might actually care about the kid he abandoned."

"But why did you wait?" Karen prodded, turning in her seat to face him directly. "Why didn't you come sooner?"

"Grandpa."

"Leland Pope, correct?"

Anson's head snapped back to me, panic widening his eyes. "How much do you already know?" he demanded, his voice squeaking with stress. "Why do you even want to talk to me if you already know everything?"

"But we don't know everything." Karen laid her hand on Anson's arm, causing him to flinch and pull away. "Sorry," she said uncharacteristically, pulling her hand back and raising it in a gesture of surrender.

"We don't," she continued. "We know a little about your background, but we don't know *you*. We don't know what brought you here, or why you went to work for Fowler, or what your relationship was with him."

She paused, watching him, before she played her trump card. "And I bet the police know even less than we do."

If what I'd seen before was panic, now I saw terror. Clearly Anson had never crossed paths with law enforcement—he was, after all, a child of privilege—and the idea drove out the last vestiges of resistance.

"OK, I'll tell you," he said, his voice thick, "but you gotta promise me you're not going to turn me in to the cops. I swear to you, I had nothing to do with his accident. I swear!"

"I believe you," I said. "And we'll try to help you, but you have to come clean with us." I glanced at my watch. "And you've got about ten minutes before we have to head back to the car lot."

Anson made good use of the time I gave him, talking fast as though purging himself of all the secrets he'd been holding.

He had only learned of his real parentage a few months earlier, after Leland Pope died. He'd somehow convinced himself that Cleveland was his father. Even though he knew the man wasn't married to his mother when he was born, that he had in fact been overseas for more than a year, he'd carried the romantic notion of them somehow meeting briefly and then being separated. By his mid teens he knew how foolish the idea was, but it made him feel like a "real" part of the Cleveland family and he wasn't willing to give it up.

But when Leland Pope died, Anson's mother told him the truth: she had been briefly married to a young man, a boy really, when she was still in her teens. She had quickly recognized her mistake, her father had helped her obtain an annulment if she agreed to never tell anyone about Fowler, and her never-was husband disappeared from her life. Only after he was gone did she realize she was pregnant, and even then she didn't want Matthew Fowler back in her life.

But years of feeling neglected didn't disappear overnight, and Anson wanted to know more about the man who had fathered him.

His mother had given Anson the scant information she had about Fowler, claiming she knew nothing about his life after he left her and returned to the Pensacola area. To Anson's credit he was skeptical of her professed ignorance, but he'd kept that to himself and started to investigate just who Matthew Fowler was.

"He didn't know who I was, didn't even know I existed," Anson concluded, "but I decided to come see who *he* was. I knew he wouldn't recognize the name Cleveland so I applied for a sales job. I didn't mention the name of the dealership where I worked in Tallahassee, I just used a few of the guys there as references.

"He never did find out who I was, and considering what I learned about him I'm kind of glad he didn't. I'm not sure I want anyone to know he's my biological father.

"I mean, look how it screwed up Joe."

"Joe?" Karen asked.

"Yeah. We got to be friends pretty quick." The ghost of a smile turned up the corners of his mouth for a moment. "Kind of like brothers, I guess. But the way his old man treated him, it's a wonder the guy isn't a total basket case."

"There's one thing I still don't get," I said when he finished. "If all this happened thirty years ago, and your mom married and had a good life—it looks like your family has been quite successful—why is she pushing your claim on Fowler's estate? Especially since you say you and Joe are friends. How is that going to work when he finds out you're the one claiming what he thought was his?"

Anson hesitated. After all he'd told us, there was still something he was holding back; some final secret he was hesitant to divulge.

"You gotta level with us," Karen prodded.

"She figures he owes us; her and me."

"How so?"

I waited, biting my lip, for him to answer Karen's question.

"Because of how he got started."

"Because your grandfather taught him the ropes, before Fowler hooked up with his daughter?"

"That," he said, "and how he financed his first business."

CHAPTER 28

We waited for him to continue, the hiss of the air conditioner and the low idle of the engine the only sounds in the deserted landscape.

"He got the money from my grandpa."

Karen's face registered shock, but she covered it quickly. I doubt I was as smooth, judging by Anson's harsh chuckle.

"Yeah, Grandpa gave him the money to start his first lot. Basically a bribe to not fight the annulment, to go away and never see my mother again.

"Not that I think that was much of a sacrifice. Guy wasn't exactly husband material if you ask me."

Well, that answered the question of where he got the money to start his dealership!

"Joe's mom doesn't know that, and she hasn't tried to find out what we're asking for. She just went off the deep end and she's trying to convince Joe that it's all a scam to get 'their' money."

His breathing had returned to normal, and he visibly relaxed against the seat. "It's not even her money, it's Joe's. He says the will has always said the only kids inherit, and Joe's the only kid."

133

"That we knew of," Karen commented drily. "Of course, now there's you. And who knows how many more we'll find."

Anson stiffened and Karen touched his hand. This time at least he didn't flinch. "Sorry," she said again. "Fowler had a reputation, well-deserved I'd say, and it is possible there are more kids out there."

"Maybe. But..." he hesitated.

"Joe told you something more?" I said softly, trying to hide my eagerness.

"Yeah. I think he felt like I was somebody safe to talk to. The guys at work were his dad's employees, and everybody else knew his dad or his mom. I wasn't from around here and I didn't know the family history, so...." He shrugged. "I want to think he kind of liked me, too.

"I don't know how he'll feel when he finds out who I am."

"You seem like a nice guy," Karen said. "Joe could see that, and from what he's told you, it sure sounds like he needed someone to talk to.

"But you started to say something else. Something about other kids?"

I snuck a glance at the clock on the dash. We'd been sitting more that the 10 minutes I'd promised Anson, but I didn't want to break the fragile connection we had established.

"Yeah. That. Joe told me his mom had insisted that the will specify that only legitimate children could inherit.

"I guess she had the same idea you did."

Karen nodded. "And *she* was sure Joe was the only legitimate heir, so she figured he'd take care of her."

"He would," I said. "Joe and his mom are pretty close."

"Maybe not," Anson volunteered.

Now that his resolve had been breached he seemed anxious to spill the secrets he'd been holding. I took a last furtive glance at the clock, then dismissed my concern with time. If Anson wasn't worried about how long we were gone, then neither was I.

According to Anson, Joe and Kerrie had been fighting a lot lately, mostly about Shiloh. Kerrie didn't approve of the girl, and she didn't hesitate to say so. It had become clear to Joe that his mother thought he should date someone from a "good family," which in Kerrie-speak meant one with lots of money.

A clerk in a flower shop didn't meet Kerrie Fowler's expectations, no matter how her son felt.

"Is Joe serious about her?" I asked.

Anson nodded. "Says he wants to marry her. They've dated for a couple years, I think, and he says it's time. Even has a ring picked out."

I couldn't help smiling. I liked both Joe and Shiloh, and they seemed to be good for each other. I mentally wished them well.

"I, uh, we should probably be getting back," Anson said. "They'll expect me to come back with a signed contract after all this time." He laughed weakly, acknowledging the fact that we were not going to buy a car today.

I turned around and put the car in gear. "I may not be in the market right now," I admitted, "But when I am, I know who I can come to."

Karen cleared how throat. "Actually, my husband may be looking to replace his pickup," she said. "Give me your business card and I'll pass it along to him."

I kept my gaze straight ahead as I navigated the empty streets back to the highway, but a slight grin turned up the corners of my mouth. Getting a foot in the door with the Freed clan could be very good for a young salesman.

Maybe today wouldn't be such a bust for young Mr. Cleveland after all.

We dropped Anson and the car back at the lot with a public display of regret that it wasn't quite right for us and an equally public promise to come back. I think his look of disappointment was genuine, though it could also have been a bit of remorse over how much information he had shared with us.

But instead of piling immediately into Karen's SUV, we detoured around the building to the service area. Keeping well back from the open bay doors, we watched the coverall-clad service crew crawl under and over a trio of vehicles.

The fourth bay stood empty, yellow caution tape still strung around the perimeter. With a start I realized it had only been a week since Fowler had died in that spot.

A little shiver ran down my spine at the realization.

"I managed to get a little closer than this that night," Karen whispered. "There was a car on the lift and a crowd of cops and paramedics standing around a couple crime scene techs.

"They knew Fowler was dead, so they were keeping everyone back while they documented the scene. Boomer might look like some cartoon sheriff, but he knows his job and he runs a professional department."

My mind went back to the night of Fowler's death, and my encounter with the twitchy deputy.

"With at least one exception," I said.

Without turning her gaze from the service bays, Karen made a face. "What do you mean?"

I told her about the trigger-happy Simonds and found my hands shaking as I recounted our run-in with him.

"I don't know what he would have done if Boomer hadn't come along just then."

Karen nodded slowly. "Doubt he was one of Boomer's. They called in backup from a couple of other counties and I heard Boomer wasn't real happy with some of the help he got."

I didn't know whether to be reassured or worried. It meant Keyhole Bay was in good hands, but it didn't say much for law enforcement in the area outside our little town.

As we watched, one man looked over and registered our presence. He said something to another tech and headed our way. We were about to get chased off.

CHAPTER 29

*A*s he approached I saw the name "Roy" embroidered above the pocket of his coveralls.

"Hi, Chet," I said cheerily. "How ya' doing?"

He looked confused for a minute, then broke into a grin. "Hi yourself! Doin' pretty good, how about you?"

"Not bad," I shrugged. "Sorry if we're in the way or something. Just morbid curiosity, I guess, looking at the accident scene."

Karen looked from me to Roy, pointedly staring at his name tag and then looking back at me.

Roy laughed. "First time we met I was wearing another guy's shirt." Karen nodded and Roy turned back to me, the laughter wiped from his face.

"Not likely I'll do that again.

"Terrible business. Terrible. Fowler wasn't everybody's favorite guy, but nobody deserved that. Hit us all pretty hard. Chet called off, been a no-show ever since, and it sounds like he isn't coming back."

He shook his head. "And nobody's gonna convince me it was an accident. We checked and tested those damned lifts—pardon my French, ladies—tested them every day. There was nothing wrong with that thing.

"Nothing."

"I'm curious," I said, "how do those things work? I mean, do they have a button or a lever or something? How do you control it moving up and down?"

If Roy was right and there was nothing wrong with the lift, then that would prove what Bluebeard had said. But how could someone operate the lift without Fowler knowing about it?

"There are two buttons. You hold one to move it down and the other to move it up. If you let go of the button, it stops." He shrugged. "Pretty simple."

"So Fowler couldn't have accidentally brought the thing down while he was under it?"

"Not unless he was Stretch Armstrong. The controls are several feet from the lifts just for that reason." He paused, thinking. "If I remember, the state safety guys even measured to make sure it was the legal distance."

I had a vague image of a super stretchy toy I'd seen in some of my vintage pricing guides reaching from under the lift to the controls several yards away.

"So the controls were too far away." I nodded. "But those things don't move very fast, do they? If it was coming down, wouldn't he have enough time to get out of the way?"

"Should have," Roy agreed. "And they're supposed to have sensors that will stop it if they detect something in the way.

"Nearly lost an expensive antique before we put those it. Some fool pulled up too close and one of the guys was bringing down a lift. Missed his bumper by, I swear, less than an inch.

"Fowler lit into him something fierce."

"He was pretty touchy about safety, wasn't he?" I remembered the time Fowler had caught Ernie in the service area—fortunately he hadn't seen me—and given him what-for.

"Yeah. Whatever else he was, and it sure wasn't all good, he did make sure we followed all the safety regs. Course it was likely 'cause he didn't want to get sued if a customer got hurt, or pay the time off if one of us got an on-the-job, but still..." His voice trailed off and he glanced back at the service bays, still filled with vehicles awaiting repairs.

"I better get back," he said. "Good to see you and all, but you really shouldn't be out here. Could be dangerous; too many rigs moving around with nobody expecting people to be walking around."

I nodded my agreement, and Karen and I moved off as Roy loped back to join the other mechanics.

The trip to the car lot had taken more of the afternoon than I had expected, but it had been worth it for the amount of information we had gathered.

Still, we weren't any closer to finding out what had really happened to Fowler, even though our conversation with Roy had reinforced out conviction that it wasn't an accident.

"There was one thing," Karen said as she parked in the alley behind Southern Treasures and followed me into the warehouse.

"Yeah?"

"Anson said that Kerrie didn't even bother to find out what they were asking for before she went off the deep end. That sounds like maybe they want something specific.

"In fact, the way he said it, I wonder if they'd planned to settle for far less than the half Anson would be entitled to."

"Makes sense," I said, warming to the idea. "And if Anson and Joe had become friends, maybe Anson didn't want to take his friend's inheritance when he already had a pretty good pile of his own. He seems like a nice enough guy to do that."

"Mrs. Cleveland was an only child," Karen said. "The family clearly had enough money to buy off Fowler thirty years ago, and they appear to have been successful since then, so she should stand to inherit a bundle."

"Unless he left it directly to the grandkids."

She nodded. "He left the business to the Clevelands, provided for his widow, so very possible."

"I better get back to work. Julie and Chloe are doing an amazing job, but they can't do it all. And," I groaned inwardly, imagining the nightmare that faced me, "I need to check on the progress upstairs."

Karen laughed and waved as she headed to the back door. She turned back before she opened the door. "Hey! What's for dinner tomorrow?"

This time the groan didn't stay on the inside. "Ugh! I have no idea. Jake and I better figure that out, huh?"

CHAPTER 30

I locked the back door behind her and went through the warehouse to the front of the store. There was the usual crowd of tourists, kids clustered around Bluebeard's cage, and Julie overseeing everything with cool patience.

I thought back to what it had been like, running the store without her when my annoying cousin Peter still owned half the place. It made my stomach a little hollow just thinking about how many plates I'd had in the air just a few years ago.

Sure, I was busy now, but nothing like I had been. There was still anxiety over money but that was a hallmark of any small business; I had to balance my own hours in the store with managing paperwork and ordering; and now I had my relationship with Jake, whatever that was.

Still, being my own boss, not having to listen to the opinions of an over-educated know-it-all who had never worked a single day in the store, and knowing I was building for my own future? Priceless.

Loud noises from overhead reminded me of another bit of business: my snug little apartment was undergoing a transformation of its own.

I hoped.

Rose Ann was with her grandmother today, but Julie would have to go rescue her mother soon. I held up my hand, fingers spread. "Five minutes," I mouthed. Julie nodded her understanding as I headed for the stairs.

My apartment—before the destruction—had been large enough to be comfortable for six or eight people, as long as they were friendly. Now it felt as though there were at least a dozen workmen and a couple trucks' worth of tools in the cramped space.

The sink had been gone last night, and now the refrigerator was back on the tiny balcony. Two men were pulling the last of the plasterboard off the wall that had separated my place from the attic of Lighthouse Coffee. As they exposed the framing, two more men, who looked enough alike to be a father-son team, pulled heavy wire through holes in the studs. Updating the wiring had become a "might as well" project once I decided to put in new insulation and sheetrock.

"It will be worth it in the long run," Riley had assured me. "I mean, how old is that building? Upgrading the insulation will save you money on heating and cooling. And the last thing you want to have to do is tear into it in a couple years because something broke."

I'd looked at the numbers, swallowed hard, and decided I could live on ramen for a few months if I had to. Now, as I imagined the labor hours piling up from the crowd of workmen, I wondered just how many months that might end up being.

Tim caught my eye from across the chaos and waved me over. "Will tomorrow night work to shut the water off?"

I stared at him, dumbfounded. They couldn't shut the water off! How could I run a coffee shop without water?

"We'll schedule it after Lighthouse closes," he said as though reading my mind. "Just for a couple hours. The plumbers," he gestured at yet another group of men clustered around the "wet wall"—a term I had learned to my relief meant a wall with water pipes in it, not a wall that was actually wet—where the sink had been, "want to move some pipes and it's safer if the water is turned off."

"Is four too late? Chloe can be closed up by then," I asked. "Not to be a penny-pincher, but I'd rather not run into overtime."

Tim shook his head. "Four should be fine."

I thanked him and retreated down the stairs. I could only take so much of the destruction of my home before I began to feel over-whelmed.

Halfway down the stairs my stomach growled so loudly I was sure the entire store had heard it. I made a beeline for the coffee shop, grabbed one of Chloe's ham-and-cheese turnovers, and took it back to my desk in the warehouse where I ate with one hand and pushed paper with the other.

A few minutes later Julie stuck her head into the alcove that held my desk. "I'm getting ready to go," she said.

I looked up. "I know. It's your early day, so you can rescue your mother from the toddler."

She shook her head and pointed to the clock in the corner of my computer screen. "No. Shop's closed, boss."

Apparently I'd lost track of time. Those few minutes had been two hours.

"I am so sorry! You should have reminded me."

"You were busy." She shrugged. "Besides, Rose Ann's with the Parmenters for an overnight." A faint blush colored her fair-skinned face. "I have a date."

I started to tease her about the date, then shook my head at her previous sentence. "The Parmenters? Overnight? Really?"

"Mom and I have been working on that. I shouldn't keep them from seeing their only granddaughter."

"Except that their son claimed he wasn't the father. Oh, and he tried to kill you. Tried to kill me too, for that matter."

She smiled sadly. "That was the drugs," she said. "My counselor helped me see that. And it's worse for the Parmenters. Their only son is in jail and they won't ever have another grandkid.

"It can be hard sometimes," she admitted. "I just have to remind myself that I am doing what is best for Rose Ann. I don't want her growing up without her grandparents."

"I suppose. Especially if they'll take her overnight so you can have a date." I stood up from my chair and gave her a hug. "You're an amazing mom, you know. Rose Ann is a lucky kid."

"Thanks. Now I have to run or I'll be late."

I waved her out the back door just as the phone rang.

CHAPTER 31

I considered letting it go to voicemail until I saw the number. It was Linda. Normally she would just pop over from next door.

I grabbed the phone.

"Hi, Linda. What's up?"

"Are you still at the shop?" she asked. "The door was locked."

Of course, Julie had locked up before she left.

"I'm in the back," I said.

"Okay." She hung up abruptly and I wondered if that meant I was supposed to open the front door or that she was coming through the alley in back.

My question was answered a few seconds later when she came through the back door.

"Got a minute?" she asked.

I waved to the chair across from my desk. "For you, always."

She sat down, but seemed hesitant, as though she didn't know where to start. I forced myself to be patient. Clearly something was bothering her.

The only sound for a long minute was muted thumps from

upstairs, eventually replaced by the buzzing of a text on my cell phone. Karen's face popped up with a text, *I'm at the front door.*

I made a face at the phone. She had just dropped me off a couple hours ago. What was she doing back here already?

Karen breezed into the store when I unlocked the door, heading to the back before I could even ask her why she was there, barely acknowledging Bluebeard's wolf-whistle.

She waved a greeting to Linda as she went past her toward the back door, her attention on the area around the door.

"I can't find my key card," she called over her shoulder. "I think it fell out of my pocket, and this is the only place I've been all afternoon."

I didn't bother to remind her she'd been all over Fowler's before she brought me home. She seemed certain she had dropped it in the warehouse.

To my surprise, she was right. Within a minute she sighed dramatically as she ducked down to pluck the plastic rectangle from under a shelf near the door.

"The station manager would never forgive me if he had to reprogram all the cards," she said as she came back to the desk. "I didn't notice it was missing until I left the station, and he was already gone for the day.

"Now he'll never know." She looked from me to Linda and back as though confirming our silence.

We both nodded, as Karen's expression became quizzical. "What's up?" she asked. "It looks like I might have interrupted something important."

Linda's resolute expression signaled her readiness to share what had her upset.

"I found out something about Matthew Fowler today. I thought I should tell you," she nodded to me. "And I think Karen might want to hear this too, since she's here."

I slid into my chair and Karen stood as though frozen. Something in Linda's tone sent a chill through me. Whatever she'd heard, I was sure it wasn't good.

"I was talking to my sister, Annie, about Fowler. The subject came up of his chasing after high school girls even after he graduated.

"Well," she took a deep breath, "her daughter Kat just called me. She said she didn't want to talk in front of her mother, but she heard us talking and she needed to tell somebody what she knew."

I held my breath, terrified of what I might hear next. What could a teen girl know about Matthew Fowler that she wouldn't—or couldn't—tell her mother?

Linda continued her story. "Kat's on the cheerleading squad. She told me Fowler had been hanging around the football team like he always had, but he seemed to be paying a lot of attention to one of the older cheerleaders, one of the seniors."

Karen groaned and shook her head. "Tell me he didn't…" She let her voice trail off, as though even she couldn't say what we were both thinking.

"No, no, no," Linda said quickly. "At least not yet. But Kat told me Olivia—that's her name, Olivia Parker—kept talking about having an 'older' boyfriend, and she kept hinting around that they were getting serious but they were waiting until she turned eighteen.

"Which was only a few weeks away."

The feeling of dread subsided, but I still felt icky just thinking about how close that young girl had come to being another of Matthew Fowler's victims.

That was the key. *Another* of Fowler's victims.

I knew, without the need for additional evidence, that she wasn't the only one.

"Maybe we've been going at this all wrong," I said slowly, looking from Linda to Karen and back again. "We've been looking at his history, at the people from way in his past. Just because Anson and his mother showed up just before Fowler was killed doesn't mean they killed him. Correlation, not causation.

"Maybe we should be looking for someone in his present, not his past."

Karen nodded. "What if the cheerleader's dad found out and lost his temper? I wouldn't blame him. Never mind that she was underage, but some old guy creeping on his daughter? You bet I'd be angry!

"It might even have been an accident, a fight or something got out of hand."

"OK. That's a possibility. Same goes for Kerrie. Maybe this was just the last straw. Or maybe the fact that the girl was too young to even be dating her son, much less her husband." I shivered a little at the thought. "Eewww."

Linda shook her head. "I know the dad. Jeremy Parker. He had a temper when we were kids, got to know the sheriff pretty good. But he got in one fight too many and ended up in juvie for a few weeks.

"You know the saying, 'scared straight'?

"He purely was. I don't think he could kill a fly anymore, much less a man."

She shook her head. "He'd be upset, even angry. But I can't see him hurting anyone."

"I feel the same way about Anson," Karen said. "I crossed him off my list after that first time we talked to him."

"Kerrie, though?" It was Linda's turn to shiver. "I wouldn't want to be on the wrong side of that girl. She's so sweet, butter wouldn't melt. But let me tell you, I have seen the ugly underneath when she did not get her way.

"If she was mad enough..." Now her voice trailed off as though, like Karen, she couldn't bring herself to finish the thought that was clearly in her head.

I nodded. "But if it wasn't them, who was it?"

"Couldn't it have really just been an accident without anyone else involved?" Linda asked, her voice hopeful. I loved her for that—she always wanted to believe the best of people. Well, except maybe Matthew Fowler. But everybody else? Definitely.

"No. Bluebeard insists it wasn't an accident, and he's been in a complete state since this happened. He never does that except when there's been a murder." That wasn't any kind of evidence I could take to the police, but it was enough for me.

It was enough for Karen, too. "I'm with Glory," she said.

From the darkened shop we all heard Bluebeard.

"Woman trouble!"

I looked at Linda and saw the hope fade from her gaze. "I guess you're right."

"I want to talk to the girl's father," I paused, searching my memory for the name she'd given us. "Jeremy?"

"Yeah?" A strong baritone voice floated down the stairs, startling all of us.

As we turned to look, a broad-shouldered man about the same age as Linda appeared on the staircase as though summoned by our conversation.

"Did you need something, Miss Martine?"

I recognized the older of the two wire-pullers from the chaos of the construction project overhead, and he apparently knew my name.

Linda's eyes went wide as she caught sight of the man, but she recovered quickly. "Jeremy! I haven't seen you in forever! How are you?"

"Doing just fine, Miz Miller." He seemed genuinely pleased to see her. "And you?"

"Fine, just fine." She smiled. "But what are you doing here?"

"Wiring," he answered. "Got my electrical ticket a few years back, and now I'm mostly working with my oldest boy, teaching him the trade," he added, confirming my earlier suspicion.

He turned back to me. "I'm the last one out today," he said. "The others already left. Was there something else you wanted, Miss Martine?"

I shook my head, unable to come up with a convincing reason I had spoken his name and unwilling to admit we were just discussing him as a possible murder suspect. I had a hunch that wouldn't have been a good way to start a conversation, no matter how harmless Linda thought he was.

"If I did, it purely went right out of my brain," I said with a little laugh.

Better to have him think I was an airhead than that I suspected him of murder. Much better.

He nodded, seeming to accept my excuse, and looked back to Linda. "Nice to see you again, Miz Miller. You tell your husband I said hey."

"I will," she said.

The man passed on through the warehouse and let himself out the back door.

The door closed behind him and I lowered my forehead onto the desk, feeling like a complete idiot.

Karen laughed. I raised my head and glared at her. "Not funny, Freed!"

"Ah do declare," she said in an exaggerated drawl, "Ah jus' don't know *what* I was thinkin'!" She batted her eyes at me and laughed again.

"It wasn't that bad," I muttered.

"It so was," she shot back. "Fortunately for you, it looks like he bought it."

CHAPTER 32

*W*hen Linda left a few minutes later we were no closer to a solution. We all felt like we should talk to Jeremy Parker, but none of us had any idea how to approach him without letting on what we knew about Olivia—and that wasn't our secret to share.

I suggested Linda talk to Kat, see if the girl was willing to divulge anything more about Olivia. Linda hesitated, but agreed that since Kat had taken the first step, she might tell Linda a bit more. Linda promised to call her, but that was as far as she would commit.

Karen left right after Linda, saying she had to get home because it was her night to cook dinner. The idea that she was cooking left me speechless and wondering who she was and what she'd done with my best friend.

I went up front to deal with Bluebeard and wait for Jake. I stroked Bluebeard's head as I offered him a piece of melon. "I wish you could tell me how you know this stuff," I said, adding some grapes to his food dish. "It would certainly make my life a lot easier."

"Coffee?" he said, as though asking for a bribe.

I shook my head. "Even if it would get the truth out of you I couldn't do it, old man. You know that."

"Coffee." This time it was almost a sigh, a delivery so dramatic it made me giggle.

"You can be as pathetic as you want," I told him. "But I am not going to poison you, no matter how many times you ask."

He retreated a couple steps into his cage, muttering. I couldn't make out any actual words, but the meaning was crystal clear. And profane.

I unlocked the front door when Jake knocked, and nodded toward Bluebeard's cage from which muttered curses continued to trickle. "I won't give him coffee."

Jake gave a short laugh. "He never gives up on that, does he?" He hugged me, calling over my shoulder to Bluebeard, "Take it easy, buddy. She's looking out for you."

"Trying to eat my $@#%^$$* dinner in peace," was the reply.

"Apparently his highness wishes to dine uninterrupted," Jake said, releasing me and taking my hand. "Shall we go upstairs and see what progress has been made? And perhaps you can tell me what you were up to all afternoon?"

I realized belatedly that there was a lot to tell.

Little had changed since I'd looked upstairs earlier, and I gave Jake a quick tour of the progress. At least I think it was progress. It was hard to tell.

"They're working on the wiring," I said, waving at the web of heavy wire woven through the skeleton of exposed lumber. "And tomorrow they need to turn off the water for a couple hours to do something with the plumbing."

"Good thing we're cooking at my place," Jake said, reminding me that—in addition to all the other things I had on my plate—tomorrow was my night to cook for the weekly dinner with Felipe and Ernie, and Karen and Riley.

I groaned. "We still haven't figured out what we're cooking."

"I had an idea," Jake said, his voice rising in an almost-question.

"Let's hear it," I said. "Right now I am up for anything, since I clearly can't cook here." I waved my hand at the spot where my kitchen used to be.

"How about taco salads? We can do it buffet-style, let everyone build their own bowl. Make guacamole and pico de gallo, serve it with tortilla chips, and we're done.

"Flan would be a good dessert," he continued, "but that would require turning on the oven."

He grinned at me and continued, "I might be persuaded to make tapioca instead."

He had me there. I had tasted his tapioca a few weeks earlier and it was honestly the best version of any custard I had ever eaten. Ever.

"If you will make dessert, I will do whatever you ask."

His voice dropped into a low register, and he cocked an eyebrow at me. "Whatever I ask?"

I blushed furiously as the suggestive tone. "Within reason, buddy. What kind of girl do you think I am?"

Jake laughed and hugged me close. "My kind of girl," he answered.

I let myself relax against his chest, shoving away the worries and stress for a moment before pushing myself away and looking up at him.

"Seen enough of this mess? If we're going to cook, we better get to the grocery store."

Jake nodded and we started back down the stairs.

"You still haven't told me about your trip to Fowler's this afternoon," he reminded me.

"There's a lot to tell," I said. "Just wait 'til we get home and I'll fill you in on everything."

The trip through Frank's Foods distracted us as we gathered salad ingredients and a ridiculous number of avocados. Guacamole was extremely popular with our crowd and it wouldn't do to run out.

On the drive home I began filling Jake in on the discoveries of the day. By the time I got through our encounter with Anson and Karen's and my dismissal of him as a suspect, we had the groceries unloaded and were elbow-deep in cooking prep.

"He sounds like a pretty decent kid," Jake said as he lined up the tapioca ingredients.

I stepped over and kissed his cheek before going back to chopping green onions. "He does seem like a good kid."

He pulled a large pot from the cupboard and set it on the stove top. "I think I'm going to double this. We'll have the leftovers for days, and as long as I'm going to be standing over a hot stove, we should definitely get a reward."

I had to laugh. "You just thought of that, huh? And you just happen to have the tapioca pearls already soaked overnight for a double batch?"

He dismissed my jab with a wave of his hand and changed the subject. "So is that your news for the day?" He asked as he poured the milk in the pot and added sugar.

"Oh, not even! That was just the beginning."

I tried to sum up the rest of the day while we continued working on tomorrow's dinner.

He nodded as I told him about the encounter with Roy. "So the crew doesn't think it's an accident either. Interesting."

There was more, but I stalled. Telling him about Olivia Parker was going to take his attention away from what he was doing, with predictably bad results.

I concentrated on my chopping, filling bowls with salad ingredients and stacking them in the refrigerator. I kept an eye on Jake, waiting until he had the tapioca simmering and it would only need an occasional stir for about 25 minutes.

"There's more," I said at last.

"Figured there was," Jake answered. "But you didn't seem like you were ready to tell me."

"Not if it meant distracting you from tapioca," I said.

Jake fiddled with the stove timer, then pulled a chair out from the kitchen table and sat down. "Timer's set so I don't mess it up. Now what is it you're so concerned about?"

I swallowed hard and took the chair across from him. "Linda came over after we closed." I stopped and Jake reached across the table, taking my hand in his.

"Whatever it is, it clearly has you upset. But you know you can trust me."

I nodded, took a deep breath, and told him the story as Linda had told it to us. His sharp intake of breath told me he had the same thought I'd had and I hurried to assure him it wasn't *quite* as bad as we feared.

The timer was beeping and Jake got up to stir the tapioca.

"I can see why you were upset."

"That's not all," I said.

He set the timer again and sat back down.

I told him about Olivia's father—Jeremy—being part of the crew working on my apartment. "I need to talk to him, but I can't let him know that I know about Olivia.

"I'll figure it out," I said.

I could see Jake getting ready to argue with me but the timer beeped again, saving me from his immediate objection. It was a temporary reprieve, but I'd take it.

Jake let the subject drop while we finished up in the kitchen.

Later, as we settled on the couch with the air conditioner humming quietly in the background and an after-dinner beer, he came back to it.

"Are you sure you should get into this? You know how much Boomer hates it when you get involved."

"I'm already involved, Jake. Bluebeard saw to that. Besides, Doc Frazier still hasn't released a cause of death and there's a good chance they're going to call it an accident."

Cynicism crept into my tone. "And no one is going to care much, except maybe Kerrie, and she won't care much once she has his money."

My voice softened. "And Joe. Joe will care, even though he doesn't owe his dad a thing. If Joe cares, then Shiloh cares; and if Shiloh cares, then Chloe cares; and that makes me involved."

Jake raised a skeptical eyebrow. "Really? Is that your justification?" I could see his mouth twitching slightly, as though he was trying to suppress a grin.

"It'll do for now."

Jake shook his head in surrender. "I don't suppose it will do any good to tell you to be careful."

I turned serious. "I will be. I know you worry about me, and I appreciate that. Really. But I can't just let this go, especially now that I know what he was up to."

CHAPTER 33

For once we ate breakfast at home, rather than at Lighthouse. It was a nice moment of normalcy, making me wonder if this was how life was supposed to be: waking up with the person you loved and doing normal things like having breakfast together before going to your perfectly normal job.

"This is nice," Jake said. He stacked the dishes in the dishwasher; leaving the kitchen clean had become a habit in the firehouse. Now he did it without thought and I was grateful.

Bluebeard was waiting for me when I unlocked the store.

"Out all night," he scolded.

"Upstairs is a mess," I answered, ignoring his attempt to send me on a guilt trip.

I cleaned his cage and gave him fresh food and water, then set about getting the store ready to open.

By early afternoon I couldn't wait any longer. I headed upstairs, hoping to find a chance to bring up Fowler and see how Jeremy Parker reacted.

I didn't have to try very hard.

I was still a couple steps from the landing when I heard a rumble of male voices. I stopped and listened, knowing the conversation would end abruptly if I walked in.

"Man was a pure hound dog," one voice said. "The Chamber dinner back in February? He thought I was getting the wife a drink, which I was. But I wasn't gone as long as he expected.

"His back was to me and I heard him trying to put the moves on my wife. She pretty much called him everything but a gentleman."

Someone said, "Lucky she didn't take a poke at him, knowing your wife," which was met with a chorus of laughing agreement.

"I know we're not supposed to speak ill of the dead," another voice said, "but that man should have been horse-whipped and ridden out of town on a rail."

"I know a few guys—and women too—who'd have helped."

"It wasn't just the grown women." The speaker sounded young. Jeremy's son, perhaps?

"What?"

The room grew silent and I held my breath so as not to give away my presence.

"It's true," the young voice continued. "I graduated last year, and he was always hanging around the school. Pretended he was there for the teams, for the Booster Club, but he spent way too much time trying to talk to the cheerleaders.

"Got to the point some of them would hide in the girl's locker room whenever he came around. Probably a few of them would have been happy to see him gone."

"Still wouldn't wish an accident like that on anyone, even him." The new voice sounded strained. "I was on the rescue crew that night. Nobody deserved that."

I waited another minute, hoping for more, but the last comment seemed to have killed the conversation.

I gave up and walked up the last few steps to see how the work was progressing.

Little had changed, though it was clear work was taking place. More wires snaked through the walls, pipes were laid out on the floor, the refrigerator was nowhere to be seen, and everyone seemed completely absorbed in their tasks.

Tim noticed me come in and picked his way across the room to me. "Coming along nicely, Miss Glory. Don't forget we're turning off the water at four tonight."

"Sure thing." I told myself I hadn't really forgotten. But I would have to go down and alert Chloe.

I passed through the gap into the space above Lighthouse, skirting around the father-son team who were starting to run wires into metal boxes nailed to the wall studs.

"Jeremy, right?"

The father nodded. "Hi, Miss Glory. Doing okay?"

"Fine, thanks."

He gestured toward the younger man. "This here's my son, Jackson."

"Glad to meet you." I started to extend my hand, then realized they were both wearing heavy leather gloves and let it drop. No reason to interfere with their work.

"Nice to meet you too."

Yes. That had been the voice talking about Fowler hanging around the high school. I quickly changed my mind about talking to Jeremy— his son would likely provide a lot more information, and I doubted I would have to betray Kat's confidence in the process. As for interrupting their work, I was paying for their time, wasn't I?

Filing that information away for later, I headed for the stairs to tell Chloe about the water shutoff. Better to let her know before she started something she wouldn't be able to finish.

I stopped at the top of the stairs, a plan forming in my brain. "Jackson," I said, turning back to look at the young man, "Since we're closing a little early, I think there are some pastries that shouldn't go to waste. Can you give me a hand and bring them back up for the crew?" I waved my hand in the direction of the workmen. "If your dad doesn't mind?"

I figured Jeremy wouldn't dare object, not when the whole crew heard me offer them fresh goodies from the best bakery in town.

Jeremy nodded.

Jackson stripped off his gloves and set them on top of an open toolbox. "Probably should wash my hands," he looked back toward the bathroom on the Southern Treasures side of the building, the only place upstairs with running water.

"There's a hand-washing station in the kitchen," I said. "Follow me."

I waited until we were nearly to the bottom before I spoke so we wouldn't be overheard.

"Sounds like you weren't exactly a fan of Matthew Fowler."

Behind me I could sense Jackson stiffen.

"It's okay, I wasn't either," I assured him without turning. "Yeah. I overheard you talking, but I already knew the guy was a creep."

I risked a quick glance over my shoulder and smiled in what I hoped was a reassuring way. "My mama told me not to speak ill of the dead, but that doesn't make much sense with someone like that, does it?"

I stopped at the bottom of the stairs and waited for him to come down the last couple steps. "I mean, dying doesn't make the guy a saint."

Jackson looked at his feet, and nodded. "He wasn't a nice guy, even if some people didn't believe that."

"You were friends with one of the cheerleaders." I knew one of the cheerleaders he'd been talking about was his sister, but I wasn't going to let on that I knew.

At least not yet.

He nodded again.

I showed him the hand-washing station and waited while he cleaned up. He wasn't saying much, but at least he was listening and responding, which was enough for now.

I waved toward the front of the store. "Let's get some goodies for the guys, shall we?"

Chloe was ringing up an order for a young couple, but the rest of the shop was empty. Not something I was usually grateful for, but I didn't usually have my place torn up and the water turned off either.

She finished and turned around to us, an expectant look on her face.

"They're going to turn off the water at four," I said. "Since you have to close a little early, I figured we might have some leftovers that can go to the work crew."

She reached under the counter and handed me a couple pink bakery boxes. "Sure thing. You want to do this while I get the kitchen ready to close down?"

One of the many reasons to treasure my manager: no drama.

I took the boxes, thanked her, and she disappeared into the kitchen.

I gave Jackson a box, took one myself, and grabbed the serving tongs from the case. I put some scones and a few muffins in Jackson's box, then opened the other side of the case and began filling my box with cookies.

"Sounds to me like maybe some of the girls didn't think Fowler was such a creep," I said, trying to keep my voice casual.

I added another muffin to his box. "We won't sell these," I said. "You guys might as well take some home and share with your families."

I turned back to put another cookie in my box, dragging out the process as long as I dared. "You have a sister, don't you?"

"How did you know that?" He seemed more puzzled than alarmed, but his tone was wary.

"Somebody mentioned her to me." Another muffin. "It's Olivia, isn't it?"

"Yeah."

Another cookie.

Time was running out, and Jackson might be catching on to my bribery attempts. There wasn't much room left in the boxes. Probably my last chance.

Might as well go for broke.

"She's the one you were worried about," I said softly. "Wasn't she?"

I added another cookie and closed my box. I took the second box from Jackson and deliberately focused on folding and closing the lid, leaving him alone with his thoughts.

I risked a quick look up at his face. I could see he was closing down, withdrawing.

"Your dad doesn't have to know," I added in a near-whisper.

That broke his reserve.

"He already does." The anguish in his voice was so intense I backed up half a step.

I set the boxes on top of the counter and quickly poured a couple cups of coffee, handing one to him. I gestured toward the corner table, the one I usually shared with Jake in the morning.

"Sit down for a minute, why don't you?" I said. "If anyone says anything about your time, I will take care of it. I'm paying the bills here, after all."

The kid sank into a chair, the coffee cup clutched so tightly his knuckles turned white. "He already knows."

His voice was so low I almost didn't hear it.

I sank into the chair across from him, the boxes of goodies ignored for the moment. "He does?"

Jackson nodded, not lifting his eyes from the coffee cup.

"Is that why you're so upset? Because he found out?"

He was just a kid. I shouldn't push him. But it seemed like he wanted to talk and didn't know who to trust. I forced myself to sit still and stay quiet while he worked it out for himself.

From the kitchen I could hear Chloe closing things down for the night. The dishwasher started up, racing the water shutoff.

I waited, hoping Chloe would stay busy in the kitchen.

Jackson knuckled his eyes and finally looked up. The kid looked like he wanted to cry, and I realized how distressed he was.

"Or is it something more?"

He shook his head, whether in response to my question or just to the situation in general I wasn't sure.

"He was there."

CHAPTER 34

"*A*t Fowler's?" I tried to keep my voice calm. That was definitely not what I had expected; I had already taken Linda's word for Jeremy's innocence.

"Yes. I saw him. He hit the guy."

Oh. My.

No wonder he was so upset.

"He hit Fowler?"

He nodded. "That was all I saw. Dad was really mad, yelling at him to stay away from my sister, and then he punched him. I've never seen my dad hit anyone. He never even spanked us when we were kids."

I wanted to reassure him, to tell him his dad wasn't responsible for Fowler's death. But could I do that without making him confront the fear that Jeremy *was* responsible?

As I hesitated he plowed ahead. "I saw him punch Fowler. He went down and dad just walked away. But what if he went back? Or Fowler got up and fought with him?"

"I really doubt that, Jackson. Someone I trust completely told me your dad wouldn't hurt anyone. I mean, he might have been really mad, but he walked away. Right?"

"Yeah." The kid brightened a little, grasping the slender thread of hope. "He got home before me even, and he didn't look like he'd been in a fight. He wasn't even late for dinner."

I nodded. "Something happened after your dad left. I'm sure of that. The lift malfunctioned or whatever. But I don't think your dad did anything wrong, and you really don't either, do you?"

He smiled and sipped his coffee, relief visible in every move. "No, I really don't. But it was hard not to be scared.

"I have never seen him so mad. Even when I wrecked his car my junior year."

"I can't blame him for being mad," I assured him. "Fowler was a total creep and had no business being around your sister. But I believe your dad didn't have anything to do with whatever killed Fowler."

"Thanks, Miss Glory," Jackson said. He looked nervously at his watch and downed his coffee. "I better get back upstairs before somebody thinks I'm not pulling my weight. There's already people think I only got my job 'cause of my dad."

We took our cups to the kitchen before I sent Jackson back upstairs with the pink boxes full of pastries. I gave him a handful of white bags and tissues so the guys could take goodies home with them. "Give them free muffins and they will forget all about how long you were gone," I said with a chuckle.

I stayed downstairs to talk with Chloe for a few minutes about the shutdown and apologize for not telling her sooner. I gave her a list of the things I'd taken from the case and told her to charge them to my personal account. I worked very hard to keep the accounting for both stores separate from my personal finances. Especially since I was using bakery items to extract information that had exactly zero to do with the store.

Chloe shook her head. "Even when it's stuff I would have to put at day-old prices tomorrow? Miss Glory, you are the most honest person I know."

I thanked her for the compliment, but deep down I knew better. I was a nosy person exploiting a scared young man to get information about a police investigation that was none of my business—just ask

Boomer! But I also knew I couldn't let it go—not as long as Bluebeard (and Uncle Louis) were telling me it wasn't an accident.

I left Chloe to finish closing up and walked through into Southern Treasures.

I stopped to check on Bluebeard, who was busy charming a gaggle of young women who looked like they were starting a bachelorette weekend a little early. He was cooing at the "pretty girls" when I walked up. He gave me a look and then turned back to the girl at the center of the group, the one I assumed was the bride.

His wolf-whistle was low, but distinct. The girls erupted in gales of laughter, and he looked back at me as though daring me to reprimand him. He could be a real brat sometimes.

"Manners!" I said. He muttered at me and the girls had another laughing fit.

I smiled at them. "Please excuse Bluebeard. He is a terrible flirt, but he usually has better manners."

They waved away my apology and threw kisses at Bluebeard. "He's adorable," one of the bridesmaids said. "Nicer than most of the men we meet."

"Except for Marshall," the bride said. She looked over at Bluebeard. "Sorry, sweetie," she waved the glittering diamond on her left hand. "I am spoken for."

Bluebeard loved the attention. He hung his head and made a very human-sounding sigh, playing to his crowd.

"Behave yourself," I said to him and walked away. The girls were having a good time with him, there weren't any kids in the store, and I knew I had to pick my battles. I beat a strategic retreat.

I signaled to Julie that I was going across the street and let myself out onto the sidewalk.

Warmth radiated from the concrete, a warning that serious summer heat was coming. Traffic had picked up in the last couple weeks and I had to wait a minute for a break to cross the street.

Beach Books was busy, customers talking quietly in the aisles as they scanned the titles for their vacation reading. Jake was behind the counter, ringing up the purchases of an admiring pair of thirty-some-things. I couldn't blame them—retired or not, he still looked like one of those firefighters on a fund-raising calendar.

I waited until he was through with his customers before I slipped behind the counter and hugged him.

"Is there anything I need to do for dinner?"

Jake looked at his watch and then back at me. "I had no idea it was so late."

"The construction crew is shutting off the water in a few minutes so I will probably close up early. Figured I'd check and see if there was anything I needed to do for tonight."

He thought a moment and shook his head. "I think we got everything ready last night. About all we have to do is put stuff in bowls and get it on the table.

"That's the beauty of a cold dinner."

I nodded my agreement. I had done cold suppers before for our dinners, when we were still trying to do traditional Southern food every week. But since we'd gone through so many recipes we had decided to branch out. Taco salads was something new for me.

Another customer came to the counter with a stack of magazines. I got out from behind the counter and waved goodbye to Jake. He had work to do, and I did, too.

I was back across the street before I remembered what I had gone over to tell him. I had let myself get distracted and hadn't told him about my conversation with Jackson.

I thought about going back, but his store was busy and I needed to get things shut down at Southern Treasures. I could fill him in on the way home.

The thought brought me up short. Was I thinking of Jake's little house as home?

Or maybe, wherever Jake was was home.

CHAPTER 35

 settled Bluebeard for the night before I crossed the street again to meet Jake for the drive to his place. Bluebeard seemed resigned to me being gone all night. Although I didn't entirely trust him alone each night, I didn't have a lot of choices while my apartment was so torn up.

"It will be better soon," I told him. Not that I believed it myself. I hadn't even gone upstairs to check things out when the crew left for the day. At least they had been true to their word; the water had been back on when they trooped down the stairs a few minutes ago.

I gave Bluebeard one last pat and offered him some grapes as an apology for leaving him alone.

He turned up his nose, er, beak, at the grapes and stomped to the back of his cage. "Trying to @^#%^&$%^ sleep."

I pulled the cover over his cage to block the light that still streamed in through the large front windows. I knew as soon as I wasn't there to witness his pout he would be back out, but I went along with his act.

I could guarantee those grapes would be gone in the morning.

Traffic was light as we headed towards Jake' place. The sun was still shining and the tourists wouldn't leave the beach and clog the roads until it was too dark to loll in the sand. Then the traffic would jam up around the restaurants for those staying in town, or on roads leading north for the day-trippers.

While Jake drove I told him about my conversation with Jackson. We were parked and in the house by the time I got through with the bare bones.

"The kid was clearly worried about what his dad might have done," I said. "I hope I did the right thing."

"I know Jeremy," Jake said. "He's one of the volunteer firefighters. Haven't worked with him a lot, but he's one of the good ones. Steady and solid, calm in a crisis. I'd trust him with my life."

That was no exaggeration. Every time the crew rolled on a call, they were putting their lives in each other's hands. Jake didn't give that trust lightly.

"But Jackson did see him punch Fowler," I reminded him.

"And he saw him walk away. He'd said his piece and warned the creep away from his daughter; he was done. That's consistent with the Jeremy Parker I know."

"That's what Linda said."

"Linda?"

I had known all along that I would tell Jake what Linda told me. I wouldn't share it with the others, but Jake was different. I told him how I knew to talk to Jackson.

"That explains a lot," he said when I was through. "I've seen guys like that; they have one brush with the consequences of their temper and quickly learn to control it.

"That's exactly how Jeremy is."

We had about 15 minutes before our company arrived, so we continued talking while we set out the salad fixings and toppings.

"But if we accept that Jeremy just punched him and walked away," I said, spilling tortilla chips into a giant wooden bowl, "then Fowler was down but alive.

"Jeremy walked away, Jackson beat feet, and Fowler was dazed, maybe, but still alive.

"So how does he end up dead just a little later?"

"The lift…"

"Nope, I don't buy that it malfunctioned," I interrupted. "Karen and I talked to one of Fowler's mechanics. They kept that equipment perfect. Whatever else he was, Fowler was an absolute stickler for proper maintenance in that shop."

Jake started to say something more, but he was interrupted by a knock on the kitchen door.

Karen didn't wait for an answer, just stuck her head in and said hi. Riley was right behind her, a six-pack of Mexican beer in each hand.

"Karen said something about tacos," he explained, setting the carriers on the counter. The bottles were frosty, and he grabbed an opener from a drawer and started popping caps. By the time he'd passed around the first four, Felipe and Ernie arrived and claimed two more.

Felipe and Ernie were immediately peppered with questions about the wedding, though they didn't have much to add to what they had told us the week before.

"Probably at home," Ernie said as he put lettuce into his salad bowl. "We thought the backyard would be nice in the fall, after the worst of the heat."

"So, November?" Karen joked.

Felipe grinned. "October more likely."

I listened to the conversation swirl around me. My news could wait until later.

Karen had teased me since she and Riley had remarried that I could be next, but I was delighted that Felipe and Ernie would have that honor. I now knew for sure that Jake loved me, just as I loved him, but marriage hadn't been mentioned and I wasn't sure I was ready for it to be.

One step at a time.

Eventually the wedding talk petered out. There just wasn't that much to say, not while Felipe and Ernie didn't have a firm date or location.

By that time we were all settled around the dining table with giant salads and bowls of chips and guacamole in the center, ready for refills.

Riley brought the second round of beers to the table and we all dug in.

As always, we spent the first few minutes of the meal talking about the food. Jake shared the recipe, such as it was, for the burger that topped the salads, and I accepted several compliments for the pico de gallo and guacamole I had made with his instructions.

Conversation drifted, as it always did, to the latest gossip, and of course Matthew Fowler's death was still the primary topic.

According to Karen, Boomer still hadn't released any more information in spite of pressure from the radio station and the editor of the *News and Times*. "He just keeps saying it's an ongoing investigation. I do know that there have been investigators from both state and federal occupational safety all over this thing, and I think Boomer's about lost his mind over having them in the middle of his case.

"From what I can tell, he would like to call it an accident and be done with it, but the safety inspectors won't let him do that yet."

I cleared my throat. "I, uh, learned something more this afternoon," I said.

"And you didn't tell me?" Karen said.

"I heard it just before I closed up," I answered. "I hadn't had a chance to talk to you yet."

She sat back in her chair and crossed her arms. "Well I'm here now," she said, "so start talking."

"There was someone in the shop with him before he died," I said. "Don't ask me exactly how I know, but he had an argument with another man and there was a witness who saw the guy punch Fowler and knock him down."

The entire table erupted as though I'd just set off a bomb, and I guess I sort of had.

"That place must have been Grand Central, with all the people coming and going," Karen said.

She narrowed her eyes at me. I was pretty sure she could guess who had punched Fowler even if she didn't know the identity of the witness.

"So you know who killed him."

I shook my head. "No, the witness said the guy knocked Fowler down and then walked away."

"That doesn't prove anything," Riley said. "He could have turned around and come back and finished what he started."

"He wouldn't have," Jake said. "Even that one punch was highly unusual."

Karen turned to glare at him. "You know who it is?" She swiveled back to me. "You told him but you didn't tell me?"

"You know who it is," I said softly. "and you know he didn't do it."

She nodded, satisfied to have her guess verified.

By now Riley, Felipe, and Ernie were about to burst.

I looked from Jake to Karen and we each nodded slightly.

"This does not leave this room," I said sternly. "We can't tell you how we know, and you absolutely can't repeat anything we tell you."

Three heads nodded solemnly. I would trust these men with my life, and I knew they would not betray their promise of silence.

Keeping names out of it as much as I could, I gave them a rundown of what we knew: Fowler's pursuit of a teenage cheerleader, her father's discovery, and his encounter with Matthew Fowler the night he died.

"Jake knows the man, and he vouches for him. A couple other people do as well. And the person who saw him punch Fowler saw him immediately afterward, so he didn't have a chance to go back and continue the fight.

"He's not our guy."

Ernie furrowed his brow and looked at Jake. "I trust your judgment, but then this means somebody came along after Fowler was down and did ... *something.*"

Jake nodded in agreement. "If Fowler was already down, it wouldn't take much to drop that lift on him."

Felipe picked at the dregs of his salad, looking thoughtful. "Up until now I had thought it had to be a man, given Fowler's size. But if he was down, maybe dazed from the first punch, it could be a woman, or a young man.

"Or a girl."

"Nope." Karen's reply was firm. "The girl he was involved with didn't know anything about this. I'm sure of that."

I wanted to ask her how she could be so positive, but I knew she had her sources. Whenever she was that sure of something she had good information to back her up.

"We know it wasn't her dad," Jake said. "And Karen says it wasn't her. What about her mother, or a sibling?"

I was convinced Jackson wasn't involved. "Not a sibling. And I don't think the mother knew, though I could be wrong about that one."

Karen spoke up in her usual take-charge fashion. "We eliminate her and her family and the first son—the one from Tallahassee—along with his family. Kerrie is hell on wheels, but I honestly don't think she'd risk doing anything like this. Not after all the other stuff she's put up with."

"Then who does that leave us?" I asked. "Bluebeard says it's woman trouble, and we think it could have been done by a woman. But we've eliminated all the women in his life."

"Probably not," Ernie said. "We all know the man's reputation. You can bet there are other women out there that had plenty of reason to hate him.

"Hate is the flip side of love," he continued. "Happens sometimes when someone you love betrays you."

"Makes sense to me. I've heard rumors about Fowler ever since I was a kid," I said. "I heard he even made a play for Shiloh Weaver while she was dating his son."

"I have the impression that she and Joe are solid," Karen said. "So who did he go after when she shut him down?"

"The cheerleader," Felipe said. "But you've already eliminated her and her family."

Jake looked troubled and I gave him a quizzical look.

"I didn't know the man as well as the rest of you," he said. "Haven't been around long enough to have a lot of history with him so I don't know the answer, but I have to wonder if the guy limited himself to one playmate at a time.

"Especially since the cheerleader was underage. Even he wasn't going to take that risk."

We exchanged looks around the table, acknowledging the truth of what Jake had said.

The problem was that none of us had any idea who Fowler's other "other woman" might be.

I caught Karen's eye and saw my own thoughts reflected in her expression.

We were going to find Fowler's other playmate.

CHAPTER 36

*K*aren pulled me aside as we were clearing the table. "Where do we start?"

I tried not to smile. I had known from the instant Jake spoke that we were going to do something, no matter what Boomer would say when he found out.

"Are we sure about the first wife?" I asked. "I mean, her son came to Keyhole Bay to learn about who his father was. If she knew how the kid felt after meeting the guy…" I trailed off. The idea sounded weak, even to me.

She shook her head. "I'd love to meet the first Mrs. Fowler, to hear her story, but this isn't about something that happened twenty or thirty years ago.

"Whatever happened in that shop was about here and now."

I nodded. "Agreed. Got any ideas?"

"Somebody must have seen him, known who his latest 'special friend' was." Her voice carried the authority of her conviction. "Who would know what he was up to? Who might have been watching him?"

"Whoever took Shiloh's job, maybe? They would know who was

coming and going from the dealership, whose calls always were put through." I tried to remember who had taken over when Shiloh quit.

"Joe."

I turned to find Ernie just a couple steps away.

"It's rude to sneak up on people," I said, hoping to deflect his entry into the conversation.

He moved a step closer and lowered his voice. "Almost as rude as interfering with a police investigation?" he said with a touch of amusement. "You know Boomer is going to be purely annoyed if you go digging around in this."

Karen ignored his taunt. "What do you mean? Joe certainly wasn't playing receptionist, was he?"

"He did whatever his old man told him to," Ernie said. "He wasn't answering the phones, but lately anybody wanted to talk to Matt had to go through Joe.

"Seemed like Matt was dumping a lot of administrative work on Joe so that he could spend more time on personal business and being a civic leader." His long fingers formed air quotes around the last word.

"Whatever went on in the dealership, most of the daily stuff landed on Joe."

Karen nodded. "And Matt could duck calls or visitors he didn't want to see by making them go through Joe." A thought clouded her face. "And with his little cheerleader finally turning eighteen, maybe he was trading in his other playmate for a newer model."

"We have to talk to Joe."

Ernie cocked an eyebrow at me. "And what makes you think he will tell you anything he hasn't already told the police?"

He had a point, but I wasn't about to admit it. "Because the police are trying to call this an accident? Maybe he doesn't want to believe he knows anything, so he's okay with that? Or maybe he thinks his old man got what was coming to him?

"There might be a lot of reasons why he hasn't said anything to the police."

"Maybe," Karen said slowly, "he wants them to call it an accident so suspicion doesn't fall on Kerrie.

"Maybe he thinks his mother did it."

We all stood in silence for a minute.

"Which is another reason for him to talk to us," I said. "Because we can honestly say we don't suspect his mom."

From the corner of my eye I caught Jake returning to the dining room with dessert and coffee. I nodded my head toward the table. "We should join the others before they start wondering what we're up to."

"Probably way too late for that," Ernie said as he walked back to the table.

Karen shrugged, and the two of us moved to the table. Whatever we might do tomorrow, right now there was tapioca waiting for us.

As we were saying our goodbyes a little later, Karen gave me a quick hug. "I'll call you tomorrow," she said, her voice promising the hatching of schemes.

Lying in bed a short while later, Jake spooned against my back, an idea hit so suddenly I jumped. Jake muttered in his sleep, a drowsy question.

I turned and patted his shoulder. "Nothing, sweetie," I whispered.

"Go back to sleep." I knew he wasn't really awake, and he snored softly in reply.

He wouldn't even remember the disruption in the morning, but I would. I had a stop to make before I tried to talk to Joe.

CHAPTER 37

I called Karen as soon as I had a minute alone. Jake was busy at Beach Books, Bluebeard was eating breakfast, and the crew upstairs were temporarily quiet.

She answered on the second ring, the hollow quality of her voice cluing me that she was on speaker.

"You in the car?" I asked.

"No. Just finishing up a story at my desk," she said, the rapid fire of her keystrokes starting up in the background. "What's up?"

"I have an idea, someone we should talk to."

"Hold on." The clicking stopped and her voice changed as she picked up her phone. "Just one more sec."

I heard a door close.

"I'm in the auxiliary booth with the feeds shut down. No sense anyone hearing this conversation.

"Go on!" she demanded, as though it wasn't her fault I had stopped talking.

"Sly. We should talk to Sly. He says he doesn't pay any attention to what goes on over there, but if this woman has been around for a while, it's possible he's seen her, or her car, or *something*."

"That seems like an awful long shot," she said. "But I suppose it couldn't hurt."

"Well, maybe he was out walking Bobo," I suggested. "Or checking the fence. Or going to his garage." I had sword Karen to secrecy before telling her about the garage full of restored vintage rides hidden in the middle of the junkyard.

"Maybe," she said, but I could tell she wasn't convinced.

"If we're going over there to see Joe anyway," I said, "seeing Sly isn't even out of our way."

We arranged to meet and I told Julie I would be out for a while but I promised to be back to cover for her at lunch.

Then I reluctantly dragged myself up the stairs to check on the progress, such as it was.

If I was honest with myself, I also wanted to get a look at Jackson and his dad and make sure the kid was okay. After the way I'd pushed him, I felt like I should check up on him.

When I walked in I was greeted with a round of thanks from the assembled crew. Apparently the treats had been a hit, and the crew seemed a bit more enthusiastic about their work this morning.

It was an extra benefit I hadn't thought about the night before when I was using the leftovers as an excuse to talk to Jackson.

I might have to try that again.

Jackson joined the chorus of thanks, then went back to the bundle of wire he and his dad were focused on. Whatever might be going on in his head, the two of them seemed as ease with each other. As I watched, the older man reached out and patted his son's shoulder in what looked like an encouraging gesture.

I hoped my reassurance had helped the young man. Least I could do.

Tim stepped over and thanked me personally. "My kids thought I was a real hero," he said with a grin. "Not often teenagers treat their old man that good."

I smiled back. "Glad to do it," I said.

I glanced around. I didn't see a lot of change, but it had been just a few work hours since my last visit. I sensed Tim was getting restless, so I headed downstairs and let him get back to work. The less I distracted him, the faster this job would get done.

And then what? I wondered as I descended the stairs into the warehouse. Was I going to invite Jake to move into the new space? And if I did, would he want to?

What if I offered and he turned me down? Even though I was practically living at his place while the renovations were being done, would he be willing to give up his place and move into mine? More importantly, would he *want* to move in together?

I shoved the thought aside. There would be plenty of time to think about it later, judging by the continuing chaos overhead.

I was waiting on the sidewalk in front of Southern Treasures when Karen's SUV swooped to a stop at the miraculously-empty curb. By the time I was belted in and she pulled out, a tourist was impatiently waiting to snag the space we were leaving.

I called Sly while we drove, and by the time we reached his gate he was holding it open with a big grin on his face.

His grin grew wider when he saw me climb out of the passenger seat with a pink bakery box. Sly took good care of himself, but he was a sucker for Miss Pansy's recipes and Chloe had mastered all of them.

"Cinnamon rolls," I said in response to the unasked question.

He nodded and rolled the gate closed. "Don't need no more busy-bodies coming around."

Karen laughed. "We're enough busybodies, I think."

"Now, I didn't say that." He chuckled. "But now that you mention it…" His voice trailed off into another chuckle.

"Come on in, ladies."

He led the way, carrying the precious box with both hands.

Once we were settled with coffee and one of Chloe's monster rolls split three ways, Sly nodded Karen's way. "Go on. What did you want to ask me?"

Karen feigned a moment of indignation. "Couldn't we just want to come by, all neighborly-like, and bring you a treat?"

Sly just shook his head and looked at her.

She dropped the pretense, and spoke quickly. "Actually, this was Glory's idea. Maybe she should tell you."

I pointed at my mouth, currently full of cinnamon roll, and Karen sighed. "Okay, since she's got her mouth full.

"We are convinced Matthew Fowler had himself a girlfriend, which is nothing new, I know.

"But we also think he may have been in the market to trade her in on a newer model. We know who the new model was, but we are trying to find out who the trade-in was.

"Because she just might have had a reason to be extremely annoyed at the late Mister Fowler.

"Extremely. Annoyed."

I swallowed and took up the explanation. "I know you don't pay much attention to what goes on over there," I said, "but maybe you saw someone coming and going a lot. Or a car there when the place was closed. Or something.

"You're outside all the time, and I know you and Bobo take a little walk every night. Are you sure you haven't seen anything that might help us figure out who it is?"

Sly shook his head. "Don't rightly think there was anyone over there more than anybody else. Some of the guys stay late to mess with their personal cars. Fowler wasn't real happy about it, but he tolerated it.

"Kept the crew happy was what he said."

I cleared my throat.

"Point is," he said, "that there were a lot of employee rigs over there on any given evening. Might be a couple in the bays, or out in the parking lot if the bays were full of customer cars. They had access to all the tools, plenty of light, and parts there if they needed them.

"Pretty sweet deal, if you ask me."

"What about last week? The night Fowler died?"

Sly was quiet for a minute, clearly deep in thought. At last he met my questioning gaze. "I might have seen Donaldson's rig over there right after the shop closed," he said slowly. "I wouldn't swear it was that night, but I saw it there within the last few days.

"And if it was that night, it wasn't late." He paused, then continued. "That was the night you brought me food, right?"

I nodded, not wanting to interrupt his recollection.

"Anna and I were coming back from the cabin, thought we might even make it in time for dinner. But she was tired so I dropped her off at home even though it was still early.

"I came back here about the time everybody was closing up and heading home, so that would have been a little after five."

"Did you tell this to the police?" Karen asked.

Sly shrugged. "They didn't ask, and to tell the truth I didn't think of it until just now. And, like I said, I don't rightly know if it was even that night. Could have been after."

"But it could have been that night," I argued. "And even if it wasn't, we ought to follow up on it, don't you think?"

"Boomer would purely laugh me out of his station," Sly replied. "If I go in there and say 'Maybe I saw something and maybe I didn't,' how serious do you think he'll take that? Especially since he thinks it was an accident."

"But does he?" Karen said. "He hasn't released a cause of death."

"He's got all them safety inspectors hanging over him. He'll get to it as soon as they let him. And then this will all get forgot and Miz Kerrie can wear her widow's weeds for a couple weeks and we will all feel sorry for her."

"I won't," Karen muttered. "She put up with him for years. That doesn't get much sympathy from me."

"So who is this Donaldson?" I asked, trying to get us back on track. "Is it one of the sales people? Or a counter guy?"

"Mechanic," Sly said. "Nice guy, actually. Name's Chet."

CHAPTER 38

*B*y the time we said our goodbyes a few minutes later, Karen had her phone in her hand and was nearly vibrating with impatience.

She tossed the keys to me as we neared the car. "You drive."

While I adjusted the seat and mirrors Karen's fingers flew over the phone. I had to remind her to buckle up before we rolled through the gate into Fowler's parking lot.

I stopped and waved to Sly as he rolled the big gate shut behind us. "Where are we going?"

Karen said, "Just a minute," without taking her eyes off the screen. Then, "Turn left."

I pulled out of the lot, muttering curses about making a left turn in the thick traffic.

Karen glanced up, realized the problem, and muttered a quick "Sorry" before going back to the screen.

"Get over to the right," she said finally. "It will be the long way around, but we can avoid at least some of this traffic."

I dutifully followed instructions, wrestling the behemoth she called a car through the way—lost tourists who meandered across lanes and occasionally stopped in the middle of the road for no apparent reason. I could imagine their conversations as couples screamed directions at each other before someone used one of Bluebeard's favorite expressions and then shrieked, "We're lost!"

Fortunately for me, Karen's experience with finding even the most obscure corners of the county kept us on the right path, and soon we were moving slowly down a street lined with cottages like Jake's. Not fancy enough for daily or weekly rentals but still solid; the kiddie pools and swing sets attested to the family residences.

"Slower," Karen said, although I was already at a crawl due to the narrow streets and parked cars. "Should be right... There. Stop!"

I nosed the SUV into the curb and turned off the engine, returning the keys to Karen. "Where are we?"

"Donaldson's. Was that even a question?"

"Not really. But what do you think we're going to do?"

"I don't know about you," she said, opening her door and climbing out. She turned back to me before she slammed the door. "But I am going to interview a potential witness."

I scrambled out the driver's side and trotted to catch up with her as she picked her way through the tricycles and toys scattered across the dry grass to the front door.

By the time we reached the porch a young woman with a toddler on her hip had come out to greet us, closing the door firmly behind her.

"Can I help you ladies?" Her tone was neutral, but there was a hint of challenge in her posture. We took the hint and stopped at the bottom of the steps.

"Karen Freed, WBBY. You're Mrs. Donaldson?"

The woman inclined her head slightly, and Karen plowed ahead. "Wondered if we could talk to you for a minute. About Matthew Fowler. I understand your husband works for him."

"Work*ed*," she said, stressing the past tense. "He quit."

"Really? I just talked to one of the other mechanics. He didn't know Chet—it is Chet, isn't it?—he didn't know Chet had quit."

"Those ol' boys in the shop don't know everything." She sighed and turned her back on us. "Don't suppose you'll go away just because I tell you to, will you?"

She shifted the toddler to the other hip and opened the front door. Even a few feet away, I could feel the rush of cool air from inside.

"Come on, then. No sense trying to air condition the whole neighborhood."

We moved quickly, before she changed her mind.

She popped the toddler into a playpen in the middle of the tidy living room and waved us to a sofa right out of the current IKEA collection. She disappeared without speaking, through a door into what I suspected was a kitchen.

Karen and I exchanged a glance, then sat silently, waiting to see what our reluctant hostess would do next.

She returned in a couple minutes with iced tea and cookies that were clearly homemade. Southern hospitality definitely lived in this home.

Settling into a matching chair across a low table from the sofa, she took a glass of tea and gestured to the table. "Help yourselves. If I have to talk about that son-of-a..." she bit her lip and then continued, "gun, we might as well be comfortable.

"I'm Clarissa, by the way."

"Gloryanna Martine."

She grinned. "The murder lady! I should have known."

"Murder lady?!?" Karen and I said in unison.

Clarissa laughed. "That's just my name for you. I've read all about you in the *News and Times*. Very glad to meet you, Miss Gloryanna."

I sat and stared, unsure what to say.

Fortunately for me, Karen was in her unflappable-reporter mode. "Well then, what do you know about that son-of-a-gun?" Only she didn't say "gun."

Clarissa's face clouded over. "He really was, you know. A complete waste of a human being.

"Not that I wanted him dead," she added hastily. "I didn't like him, and I won't pretend I am sad that he's gone, but he was a nasty piece of work."

"Your husband works—*worked*—for him, right? I thought Fowler was pretty well liked by the guys in the shop," Karen said. "I heard he let the guys use the shop after hours to work on their personal vehicles, stuff like that."

"He acted like he was doing them a favor, playing the big shot. But he managed to get some unpaid overtime out of them in the process. And he held it over the heads of every one of them.

"If somebody didn't do things his way, the whole crew would lose their 'privileges.'

"And it wasn't just the shop crew," she added, darkly.

"We know about the women in the office," Karen said quietly. "My mother worked for him once, when I was still in high school, for about two days."

"Not just them." Anger dripped from her words. "The wives."

"Are you kidding me?" I blurted out.

Clarissa shook her head. "Nope. Most of 'em were too scared to say anything, but I know he was constantly hitting on them. Even threatened their husband's jobs, some of them."

She looked at me, then at Karen, then back to me. Clearly there was something she wanted to talk about, to tell someone.

"Can I trust you two?"

I nodded and Karen answered her. "I always protect my sources," she said. "Nothing leaves this room without your say-so.

"Unless you killed him, of course."

"He wasn't worth the agitation."

Clarissa drew her phone from her pocket and set it on the table next to the plate of cookies. Looking at her face, I could see the strength there; this wasn't a woman Matthew Fowler could have bullied, even if he wasn't clever enough to realize it.

"But that isn't to say I was going to be a pushover, either."

She reached for the screen, and Karen stopped her.

"Tell us what this is first."

Clarissa explained that she and Chet had gone to confront Matthew Fowler the night he died. Beside me I felt Karen stiffen at the revelation, but she stayed silent.

"Chet was going to quit. Part of the reason was that Fowler was starting to bother me. He was getting to the point of hinting Chet's job could be affected, and we decided we'd had enough. That morning Chet took another job.

"He went and signed the paperwork as soon as he got off, then he was going to go back and tell Fowler. But Chet was pretty worked up over it all so I went along, and I told him to stay in the car and I would go talk to Fowler."

Her finger hovered over the phone. "I'm not dumb enough to think Fowler wouldn't try to cause trouble, so I set my phone to record before I went in.

"You promise this won't leave this room?"

Behind her the baby fussed. She took a cookie off the plate and handed it to him.

"Promise?"

We both nodded, and Clarissa tapped the phone.

We heard a few indistinguishable scrapes and hisses, and then a muffled whisper from the tiny speaker. She tapped it again to pause, got up from her chair and took a small wireless speaker off a shelf next to the TV.

"This might work better."

She started the playback again, and this time we could hear her clearly, even the whisper, as she gave the time and date and stated her name.

"I am about to talk to Matthew Fowler in his shop. I don't trust him, so I am recording this conversation without his knowledge or consent."

She paused again. "I didn't know if it would be a bad thing to say that or not, but I wanted to be up front about what I was doing."

She tapped the phone, and the playback continued.

I heard a door close, and Clarissa calling out to Fowler.

"In here," a weak voice called. Footsteps, and again the voice called, "In here."

More footsteps, then Clarissa said, "What the...?"

"I slipped," the other voice said. "Give me a hand."

Karen reached out and paused the recording, looking at Clarissa expectantly.

"There was an old car on the lift, and he was underneath it, on the ground. Just sitting there, kind of dazed-like."

"And you said it was 5:45 when you went in?"

"Yeah. I looked at my watch when I turned on the recorder."

Karen and I exchanged a look. We knew he hadn't slipped; the Donaldsons had just missed seeing Jeremy. And if Clarissa hadn't killed him, then someone *else* had been along after them.

That shop must have been like a scene from a Marx Brothers movie, with people coming and going and just missing each other.

Except a lot more deadly.

Karen nodded and tapped the phone.

"So, you decided to come see me?" The voice was clearly Fowler, and the implication in his tone was beyond creepy. He'd just been knocked down by the father of a teenaged girl, and here he was only a few minutes later trying to hit up the wife of one of his employees.

I was going to need a shower after this.

"Oh, yes." There was steel under Clarissa's soft Southern drawl, and if Fowler'd had any sense he would have shut up.

But he didn't.

"Come on over and give me a hand up," he continued. "Then maybe we can work something out to make us all happy."

"You know you want to."

"Well, I'm pretty happy right here."

"Come on," he whined. Muffled scrapes followed, and I could imagine Fowler trying to stagger to his feet. An "Oof" sound suggested he didn't make it.

"Dammit! Are you going to help me or not?"

Footsteps.

"Not."

Another scrape, a high-pitched curse, and then moaning.

"By the way, Chet says to tell you he quit."

Fowler's voice sounded like he was speaking through gritted teeth.

"You'll regret this, you bitch. And so will that spineless husband of yours."

"I don't think so. I have some idea how many women you've taken advantage of over the years. You won't risk being outed."

"'He said, she said.' You wanted me not to fire your worthless husband for being lousy at his job, and when I wouldn't you started telling lies."

"That's not what this says. Do you think I was stupid enough to talk to you without recording it?"

Footsteps, the sound of Fowler's moaning receding.

"By the way, Matthew," Clarissa voice was low, the anger still clear, "have you ever heard of 'Me, too'?

"Because you will."

A door closed, and Clarissa's shuddering sigh was the last sound before she stopped the recording.

"What..." I swallowed and tried again. "What did you do?"

"I paid some attention to the parts he wanted me to," Clarissa said, her voice shaky with the stress of reliving her encounter. "With the toe of my boot."

"And you just left him there?" Karen asked. From the tone of her voice, Clarissa had just moved up the respect ladder several rungs. "Weren't you worried he'd have you arrested for assault?"

"I had my recording, and some friends in the sheriff's office. Honestly, I think there might have been a lot of slow-rolling any complaint he'd filed.

"People were getting mighty tired of his particular brand of horse hockey."

CHAPTER 39

"Have you told the police about this?" I asked. I knew Boomer was going to look at this as withholding evidence. Even though I believed Clarissa, I would have to concede that he had a point and I didn't want to argue it with him.

"No." Her chin shot up. "It doesn't really have anything to do with his death, so I didn't see any reason to drag us, or any of the other families, into it."

"At some point you may have to," Karen said. "We won't tell them, but if they find out you were there..." Her voice trailed off and she shrugged. "They won't look favorably on you not letting them hear this."

"I'll think about it," she said, but I didn't think she'd think very hard.

I was in a bad spot. I couldn't tell Boomer without breaking my promise to Clarissa; and if he found out I knew before he did he wasn't going to be very happy.

By the time we were back in the SUV, the whole idea had my stomach in knots.

I glanced at my watch as Karen headed back to the car lot. Not that we expected to get anything more out of Joe, but somebody was in that shop after Clarissa Donaldson, and we needed to find out who.

"Better make this quick," I said. "I promised Julie I'd be back to relieve her for lunch."

"I have a newscast in a few minutes anyway," she said. "Do you think we could skip Joe for now?"

"Let's make sure he's there," I said, grabbing my phone. "Then we can decide."

Joe wasn't at the dealership, and the counterman who answered the phone didn't know when he would be back.

I had Karen drop me at Southern Treasures, and we promised to call each other if we heard anything. After the drama of our visit to Clarissa, it seemed so anticlimactic.

After Julie returned from lunch, I was headed upstairs to check on the progress. It was like scratching a cut that wouldn't heal; I couldn't stop myself from checking up on the crew, even though I knew I couldn't expect it to be any better.

Julie's voice stopped me halfway up the stairs.

"Telephone for you, Miz Glory. Says his name's Anson?"

"I'll take it in the office," I called back as I hustled back to my desk. What could Fowler's newest salesman want with me? I'd been clear I wasn't really in the market for a car.

"Miss Martine?" The voice on the phone was soft, as though he didn't want to be overheard.

"This is she," I replied. "What can I do for you, Anson?"

"Well, I was hoping we could stop by your shop and see you."

"We?"

"Yes. My mom's here and I was telling her about you.

"She'd like to meet you, and Mrs. Freed too, if she's available. She wants to talk to both of you. If that works for you?"

I forced myself to speak calmly, but inside I was shaking. We wanted to talk to the first Mrs. Fowler, and now she had just appeared on our doorstep.

Life was *never* this easy.

"Of course. I'd be delighted to meet her, and I am sure Karen would be too. When would you like to come by?"

"Would now be okay? She's kind of in a hurry since she's wanting to drive back home tonight."

I agreed and immediately called Karen.

"You need to get over here ASAP."

"Kinda busy," she replied.

"Anson is on his way over. With his mother."

"Why didn't you say that to begin with?"

I started to answer, but a distinct thunk told me she'd dropped the phone on her desk. I heard her call an excuse to her station manager and the jangle of keys before she picked it back up.

"On my way."

The connection cut off.

I went out front and walked over to check on Bluebeard. I still didn't know what I was going to do about him if the construction dragged on very long. That question nagged at me, but for the moment it had to take a back seat to the more pressing concern over my impending visitors.

I gave him fresh water and fed him a few grapes I'd brought from the small refrigerator in the back. "Doing okay, old man?" I said as I petted his head.

"Coffee?"

"Honestly, you're like a broken record, aren't you?" I shook my head. "You know better."

The bell over the front door rang and Karen rushed in.

A few steps behind her I saw Anson approaching the door with an older woman. I reached past Karen and held the door for the two of them.

I don't know quite what I expected of Louisa Cleveland. I suppose a slightly older version of the second Mrs. Fowler. But my immediate impression of the woman who came through the door in front of Anson was anything but.

Taller than Kerrie, and several pounds lighter, she still had the posture of the beauty queen she had been. Her hair and makeup were flawless but understated, and she wore a casual outfit of Capri pants and camp shirt that probably cost more than my entire wardrobe.

To be fair, I was pretty sure most of Kerrie's outfits cost more than my entire wardrobe, too. But casual and understated were words I would have never used to describe her.

Petite diamonds—their clarity and cut a statement of quality over quantity—sparkled at her ears and on her left hand, but she didn't wear any other jewelry. She didn't need to. Louisa Cleveland was still a woman who would turn heads no matter where she went.

I was intimidated just being in the same room with her.

For about ten seconds. Until she spoke.

"Miss Martine?" She grasped my hand in hers and shook it gently. Her tone was warm and friendly. When she said she was glad to meet me, it actually sounded as though she meant it.

I introduced her to Karen, who she greeted warmly. "I know the two of you talked to Anson and you know his background. I hoped you could give me a few minutes of your time."

"Of course," I answered. "But perhaps we can talk someplace a little more comfortable?"

I gestured toward the connecting door into Lighthouse Coffee, but our move toward the door was interrupted by a squawk from Bluebeard's perch.

"Pretty girls," he said. "Come say hello."

Louisa took a step toward Bluebeard with Anson at her heels, and I moved quickly to get between them and the bird. I wasn't sure how he would react to anyone connected to Fowler.

He behaved himself for the most part, as I gave them each a shredded-wheat biscuit to feed him. But he kept cocking his head and looking hard at Louisa, as though he should know her.

I got them moving as quickly as I could, calling over my shoulder to Julie that I would just be next door if she needed me. She just grinned and waved me on.

It occurred to me that there should be a raise in her future. Soon.

Within minutes the four of us were gathered around the table against the back wall, with iced coffees and a small plate of Chloe's goodies.

The shop was busy, but most of the customers were picking up to-go orders and no one paid attention to us as we settled in.

Louisa, as she had insisted we call her when we were introduced, sipped her coffee then set it down in front of her and leaned forward.

"The reason I wanted to talk to you was because Anson said we could trust you. He said you know who he is and why he was here, and you hadn't told anyone."

I tried not to flinch. We *had* told Jake, and Riley. Or did partners not count when it came to keeping secrets?

She went on.

"I want to talk to Mrs. Fowler. The current Mrs. Fowler." She took a bite of a cookie and flicked an imaginary crumb from her immaculate shirt.

"To be honest, I don't even know exactly *why* I want to talk to her. I suppose I want to know…" Her voice trailed off and she shrugged. "Not even sure what I want to know.

"Mostly I want Anson to find the answers to his questions."

Anson reached out and patted his mother's hand where it rested on the table. "I don't have very many questions left, Mom. I could see why you dumped him."

"But I didn't. You know that. Grandpa bought him off, and he was happy to be bought off.

"I just agreed that he should have to pay us back."

"And now?" Karen asked. "According to what we have been told, Anson has a claim to half the estate."

Anson shook his head. "I don't need his money. My granddad and my dad have seen to that.

"But at this point Mrs. Fowler has got it in her head that we're trying to steal something that's hers—and it isn't, it's Joe's. I just want her to stop saying those things."

"I was hoping," Louisa said, "that you could tell us something about her that might make it a little more productive to talk to her.

"My lawyer says I should just leave it to him, but I was hoping I could just talk to her instead of us waving lawyers at one another."

Karen took a sip of her coffee and met Louisa's gaze. "Are you sure you want us to tell you what we know? Because I for one do not believe you should never speak ill of the dead, no matter what my Memaw told me."

"Remember, that was the guy who left me because my daddy wrote him a check. Not much you could say about him that I haven't already thought.

"And really, I want to know about his wife."

Karen nodded. "Okay. But you can't talk about one without talking about the other. They were a pair."

"A pair of mules in horse's harness," I muttered.

Louisa's lips curled in a knowing smile. "I've seen a few of those around," she said. "It's a pretty common type."

Karen cleared her throat and took control of the conversation. She briefly outlined what we had learned about the Fowlers and the history of their marriage.

"Like I said, Kerrie always found out about Matt's extracurricular activities, and she always stayed with him.

"Usually that reconciliation happened right after the delivery of a new Cadillac, or a gaudy diamond bracelet, or a trip somewhere she could brag about.

"Which brings us to the last few weeks."

She paused, and I knew she was editing the information we had received in confidence. Karen might trust Louisa and Anson, as I did, but she protected her sources. "There were always rumors, but whatever he was up to, Kerrie was going to find out eventually. Then the only question was how much it was going to cost him to placate her."

"Was there anything specific?"

Karen and I exchanged a glance and she shook her head almost imperceptibly. "Nothing we know for sure," she said. "Just more of the usual stuff."

"Well, maybe there was." Anson spoke hesitantly. "Joe told me his mom had been pretty stressed out the week or so *before* his dad's accident."

"Her fault."

Bluebeard's agitated screech interrupted the conversation.

I jumped up from the table and ran across the shop to the connecting door.

I reached Bluebeard's perch at the same time as Julie did. Behind me I could hear running and I knew Karen was only a few steps behind me.

"Whose fault?"

"Hers."

"Which her?" I knew everyone was listening, and Bluebeard's secret wasn't going to stay secret, but I didn't care. I could deal with the fallout later.

Right now I needed to know what he was trying to tell me.

"Not an accident."

And there it was.

The thing he had been hinting at all along.

Fowler's death—just like the others—wasn't an accident.

CHAPTER 40

I calmed the frightened bird as best I could. I tried to talk to him, to get something more out of him.

"No accident," I agreed. "But who? Who's fault?"

"Go see her," he said. "You'll see."

He retreated to the back of his cage, still shaking and muttering, "Go see her," but wouldn't elaborate; he never did.

Louisa and Anson stood and stared, looking from me to Bluebeard and back again.

Louisa peered into the cage and murmured something softly to him. She got his usual reply.

"Trying to #%^$*$% sleep here."

Julie reflexively glanced around the shop, but fortunately there wasn't anyone within earshot. In spite of everything, Bluebeard still had impeccable timing.

"Who are you supposed to go see?" Julie asked.

I shook my head and tried to dismiss Bluebeard's outburst. "Who knows? Just some random parrot freak out."

"Glory," concern filled her voice, "if Uncle Louis thinks you need to go see someone, you need to go.

"I'll take care of things here."

Her mouth turned up at the corners. "You thought I didn't know? Everybody knows." She rolled her eyes at me, then nodded toward the door. "Go. We can talk later."

"Mrs. Fowler's?" Anson asked. He dug a key ring from his pocket and unlocked the new Tesla sitting at the curb in front of Southern Treasures. "We can take my car."

He didn't ask for directions. The on-board navigation system did a far better job than either Karen or I could have done from the back seat. and Anson threaded his way through the thickening Friday afternoon traffic with practiced skill.

We turned into Fowler's street and drove alongside a tall brick wall topped with decorative—and defensive—wrought iron railing. But when we reached the gate it stood open, inviting us to make our way up the winding drive to the brick-lined porte cochere in front of the main house.

A sleek, cherry-red Cadillac sat out front with custom plates that read "KERRIE," just in case there was any question who's flashy ride it was.

A grey, late-model sedan nosed in front of it, as though the driver had slid to a stop and tried to block the path of the Caddy.

The lights on the Cadillac flashed and the rear deck rose slowly. Kerrie herself emerged from the front door to our left, wheeling two large suitcases toward the car. A massive hobo bag bounced against her right hip with each step of her towering heels.

Lights blossomed to life in the gaping trunk, illuminating more luggage, all of it plastered with a designer logo.

Subtlety had never been one of Kerrie Fowler's virtues.

Behind Kerrie I spotted Joe, running to catch up with his mother. I opened my door in time to hear him arguing with her.

"Mom, you know how this is going to look! You can't leave yet." His voice took on a pleading tone. "Please, Mom. Just give the lawyers a little time to work this all out. Then you can go wherever you want.

"I swear, Mom. I'll buy you any cruise you want, send you wherever you want to go. But you can't leave just yet."

He reached for her arm. "Just give me some time."

Kerrie swatted his hand away. "No. I've waited long enough, and I am tired of waiting. I've got a credit card and my car, and I can go anywhere I damn well please!"

She struggled with the larger of the two suitcases, trying to heave it over the bumper into the trunk. "Aren't you even going to help me with this?" she demanded.

Joe stood his ground. "No. I'm not going to help you make more trouble for me," he said. "You've done enough of that already."

In front of me, Louisa's door swung open and she stepped out into the driveway, holding her hand up to shield her eyes from the sun.

Joe and Kerrie both swiveled their necks to look at her, as though just noticing the car full of people in their driveway.

"Can I help you?" Joe asked, confused to see a strange woman standing in his driveway, looking for all the world like she owned the place. "Anson? What are you doing here?"

Anson moved across the front of the car to stand between Joe and his mother. "Hi, Joe. Sorry to barge in like this, but we were hoping to get a chance to talk to you.

"This is my mom, Louisa Cleveland. Mom, this is Joe Fowler, the guy I've been telling you about."

Drilled-in manners took over and Joe stepped forward to take Louisa's offered hand. "Glad to meet you, ma'am."

"Louisa, please. Anson's told me so much about you."

Joe shifted uneasily. "Very sorry you had to see that. My mother's not herself right now, I'm afraid. My dad's death has hit her very hard and she's under a doctor's care, so she isn't thinking too clearly right now."

He glanced past Louisa to me and Karen, hanging back while the family drama played itself out. "Miss Glory, Miss Karen! It's always a pleasure to see you, but why are you here?"

"They're with me because I asked them to come along," Louisa drew his attention back to her with the smoothest lie I had ever heard.

Or maybe she had intended to ask us to come along and it wasn't really a lie at all.

Kerrie had managed to get the suitcase in the trunk where it leaned unsteadily against another bag. Now she picked up the smaller bag and manhandled it into an empty spot in the trunk.

The beeping of the remote caught all our attention as the trunk lid lowered into place and locked with a solid click. Up to now she had not spoken to any of us, or even acknowledged our presence.

"Move your car, Joe," she commanded, still ignoring us.

"Mom, we have company right now. Just hold on a few minutes. Anson's mom came all the way from—" He stopped and looked at Louisa. "Where did you say you were from?"

"I didn't say," she replied with a smile. "But I drove over this morning from Tallahassee."

At the mention of Tallahassee, Kerrie whirled to look at Louisa and took a step toward her.

"You! You're the one that's telling all those lies, trying to steal everything we've worked for. You're the reason I can't get my money and leave this godforsaken place."

"Mom," Joe said warily. "We don't know that."

"Of course we do. Why do you think this little weasel," she pointed a trembling finger at Anson, "came to work for your father? Why he pretended to be your friend?"

She took another step toward Louisa. "Because his lyin' mama saw a chance to try and steal from us."

She pawed through the depths of her hobo bag without taking her eyes off Louisa. "Well, I know how to deal with trespassers and thieves," she yelled.

I expected her to come up with her cell phone and threaten us with the police. I expected I might even have to explain to Boomer why I had come along with the Clevelands to Fowler's house. I expected that maybe Louisa Cleveland would stand by her story that she had asked me to come along.

What I didn't expect was the gun.

"Well, you're not going to get away with it!"

We all froze. For an instant I was back in Fowler's lot, in the dark, looking down the barrel of a gun the size of a cannon.

Seconds ticked by in silence. In the distance I heard the click-click of a sprinkler.

"Mom." Joe spoke softly as though afraid to break the spell that held us all in place.

"I can't let her get away with this."

"Mom, nobody's getting away with anything. You have my word." He slid a careful step in her direction. "Just put the gun away. We can get Boomer to deal with them."

"What's he gonna do?" The gun wavered in her hand, as shaky as the deputy's had been the night her husband died. "He won't even say it was an accident and let this be over."

"He will," Joe said, sliding another step. "He will. Just as soon as those government people get off his back."

The gun swung away from Louisa and toward Karen. And me.

"What about them? They're such nosey parkers, they're never going to leave us alone." She pointed it at each of us in turn. "Can he make them all leave me alone?"

Even with my knees feeling like jelly I noticed her shift from "us" to "me." Was she cutting out Joe?

"He will. You know he doesn't like them nosing around either. He'll make them stop, for sure."

Joe slid another half step and I tried to gauge the distance between them.

It was clear to me he was going to try and stop her.

If she didn't kill us in the process.

Kerrie turned the gun back on Louisa, who stayed as still as one of the marble statues on the porch.

The move placed Kerrie at nearly right-angles to Joe. I saw the instant of decision on his face a split-second before he made his move.

Kerrie sensed the motion on her left and swung toward him. Her movement drew her finger tight on the trigger as she turned toward her son.

CHAPTER 41

*A*t that range the shot deafened me. I looked at Karen, but couldn't hear what she was saying. She pointed toward Joe.

I followed her pointing finger, afraid of what I would see.

Kerrie sprawled against the car, rocked back by the unexpected kick of the revolver.

Looking past her I saw Joe on the ground. Anson curled next to him, a slash of red across his upper arm. Anson gestured to Joe, who nodded, and the two men scrambled for relative shelter under the Caddy.

Kerrie struggled to her feet, the gun waving wildly as she tried to regain her balance.

I ducked, terrified of where the next shot might go.

In my head I screamed at her to stop, but terror froze my throat and I couldn't even breathe.

My hearing returned a bit, and I could hear Kerrie's screams as though muffled by extreme distance.

"I couldn't let him ruin everything. He was going to lose it all with his stupid underage girlfriend if I didn't stop him."

I risked a quick look at Karen.

Her eyes wide, she mouthed the words "We've got her."

Considering who was holding the gun, I didn't believe her.

Kerrie was back on her feet. She held the revolver clenched in both hands but couldn't keep it steady as she turned her attention back to Louisa.

"Kerrie." Karen's voice wavered.

The gun barrel swung back toward Karen and she paled.

"Kerrie," she said again. "You don't want to hurt anyone. We know that. You just want to go without anyone bothering you.

"Right?"

Kerrie clutched the gun tighter, her finger once again on the trigger. Even from a few feet away, I could see her knuckles turn white with the force of her grip.

Her eyes darted between me and Karen and Louisa as though she couldn't decide which one of us was the biggest threat.

"You!" She focused her rage toward me. "You're the nosy one; the one that just couldn't leave it alone. You won't let me go."

"I'm the reporter," Karen said, drawing her attention. "I'm the nosy one. I can make sure no one bothers you. Including her."

"No. She's the one that's been sneaking around, talking to people."

I watched her finger tighten on the trigger, unable to look away, but she didn't fire.

She backed up against the car, shifting her feet as though trying to find a way to brace herself for another recoil.

The sound of a distant siren reached us. Kerrie, momentarily distracted, looked up as though she could somehow see the source of the sound.

I scrambled to the left, trying to find my way around the car without taking my eyes off Kerrie. I had no desire to turn my back on a crazy woman with a loaded revolver.

Louisa's kick came out of nowhere.

The gun fired, shattering an upstairs window.

I ducked.

The gun ripped itself from Kerrie's grasp and tumbled a few feet away.

Kerrie crumpled to the ground, her right hand cradled against her waist. She moaned in pain as Louisa roughly grabbed her shoulder and turned her face down onto the driveway.

Joe and Anson scrambled out from under the Caddy and Joe went to his mother's side, his face twisted with grief and loss.

Louisa's face softened at the sight of his pain, but she didn't loosen her grip on Kerrie.

"I had to do it," Kerrie wailed. "I put up with so much, and he was going to make me lose it all over some lovesick teenager."

Anson spotted the gun, kicking it farther away from Kerrie and positioning himself next to it.

I braced my hand against the hood of the Tesla and stood up, hoping my wobbly knees would hold me.

Beside me Karen did the same, as the siren grew louder.

Two sheriff's cars skidded to a stop behind the Tesla and Boomer leaped from the passenger side of the lead car, followed by his driver. Both men had their weapons drawn, Behind them the second car braked and another pair of deputies jumped out.

Five pair of hands shot into the air, but Louisa remained straddling Kerrie's back, pinning her to the ground.

Boomer's driver ran across the lawn toward Anson, who quickly backed away from the gun. "Didn't want her getting ahold of it again," he said.

The deputy didn't answer, just stared at Anson as he moved farther away, his hands still in the air.

Boomer holstered his weapon, the three deputies following his lead, and gave me a disgusted look.

"Should have known you'd be here," he said. He turned to look at Karen, "And you, too."

Joe got to his feet. "I'm the one who called," he said.

"One of 'em," Boomer muttered. "Phones lit up like a Christmas tree, callers complaining about somebody shooting in the city limits."

We all tried to talk at once, but Boomer shouted us into silence.

"Ma'am," he addressed Louisa, "would you please get off Miz Fowler and let her get up?" The words sounded like a question, but the tone was clearly a command.

Louisa took her knee off Kerrie's back and scooted a couple feet away, her movement slowed by reluctance. "Just so she doesn't try to shoot me again."

"She tried to shoot you?"

Again, a chorus of voices.

Boomer shot a warning look around the circle and the hubbub died down.

"Ma'am?" he said again, looking at Louisa. "Just who are you?"

"I'm Louisa Cleveland, by the way. From Tallahassee. You can check my ID." She gestured toward the Tesla. "My purse is in the back seat."

Kerrie groaned as she rolled over. Her right arm didn't work right, and she clumsily pushed herself into a sitting position with her left.

"There isn't a gun in it," Louisa added.

Karen snickered and Boomer glared at her.

He nodded for one of the deputies to retrieve Louisa's purse, then turned his attention back to the two women on the ground.

"You say Miz Fowler tried to shoot you?" Disbelief tinged his question.

"I didn't!" Kerrie protested. "She trespassed on my property and assaulted me! Look at what she did to my arm."

At a gesture from Boomer, one of the deputies approached Kerrie and helped her up. He looked at her useless right arm and gave Boomer a nod.

"We got medical on the way," the deputy said. "We'll get that taken care of."

"Hang on," Karen said.

Boomer looked at her, tensing when she moved her hand toward her pocket. "Just getting my phone," she said. "You'll want to hear this."

He snatched the phone from her hand.

"Should have known," He said, shoving it toward the other deputy. "Impound this until we can see what's on it."

"Hey!" Karen shouted. "You can't listen to anything without a warrant."

Boomer sighed.

"But I'll play it for you," Karen said. "If you give it back."

"Don't believe anything she says," Kerrie whined. "They were trying to cause trouble. I was just defending myself."

Boomer shook his head. He looked over at Kerrie. "We will get you to the hospital and get that arm looked at and then you can tell me your story.

"In the meantime we are going to take the rest of this circus down to the station and get this sorted out."

CHAPTER 42

*T*here was no arguing with Boomer once his mind was
made up.

Kerrie was transported to the hospital with instructions for a
deputy to stay with her until she could be brought to the station.

The rest of us were separated and told not to talk to one another,
while Boomer arranged for each of us to be taken to the sheriff's
station and isolated from the others.

I ended up sitting at an empty desk in the patrol office, with Anson
at another desk across the room. Boomer's driver stationed himself
between us and occasionally shot warning glances our way if he
thought we might be about to say something.

He took his job very seriously.

Boomer had personally taken Karen in first, her phone still firmly
in his control. I hoped he would let her play back the encounter in
Fowler's driveway without incident.

If they got into a confrontation she'd refuse him permission to
hear the recording and we would all be in for a very long night.

They must have worked it out, though, because Boomer eventually
emerged from the small interview room with a grim expression.
Karen followed in his wake and made a beeline for the door.

Boomer ignored all of us and went directly to his office. He picked up the phone from his desk and I could hear him issuing orders. He hadn't bothered to close the door, and I didn't believe for a second that it was an accident.

"Go by Judge Johnson's house," he said, "and pick up the search warrant for the car and the house. I'll have a crew meet you out at Fowler's house.

"I'm sending Sherman to the hospital to make the arrest."

He emerged from the office, shaking his head as though he still didn't believe what he'd heard.

"Go home," he said to Anson.

He turned to look at me. "You too. I'll deal with you later."

Karen was waiting for us outside, Riley and his pickup idling at the curb. "Climb in," she gestured to Anson. "Let's go get your car before Boomer has it towed.

"He's in a lousy mood."

It took Anson several minutes to talk his way through the search team at Fowler's, but eventually they let him retrieve the Tesla.

He drove a few blocks, then pulled to the curb. Riley parked behind him and Anson got out and came to the passenger door.

Karen lowered the window and Anson propped his arm on the sill. "Thanks for the lift," he said.

"You okay?" Karen asked.

"Better than my brother. I'm the only family he's got left now, and he doesn't even know it."

He stepped back and patted the windowsill. "Looks like Mom and I need to have a long talk with him. If he'll let us."

"Give him time," I said. "Losing your parents is hard, no matter how old you are."

I stopped. No sense in telling him how I'd learned that lesson.

Anson nodded and went back to his car.

"Nice guy," Riley said.

"Um-hmm," Karen said.

A few minutes later, Riley deposited me in front of Southern Treasures. The store was dark with just the security lights glowing dimly. True to her word, Julie had taken care of things while I was gone.

Julie! I remembered what she'd said before I left. *Everybody knows.*

CHAPTER 43

owler's memorial was a subdued affair.

With Kerrie in the hospital, a host of doctors assessing her mental state following her confession, responsibility for the arrangements fell to Joe.

The chapel was small, the crowd smaller. Joe greeted us at the door, Anson standing on one side of him and Shiloh on the other.

Louisa stood back a few paces, like a lioness guarding her cubs. Beside her, a handsome older man laid a protective arm over her shoulders.

In the week since the confrontation in Fowler's driveway, James Cleveland had spent most of his days in Keyhole Bay, helping his wife and stepson settle their claim on Fowler's estate. From what I had heard, Anson had been extremely generous with his half brother.

According to Chloe, the Clevelands had taken Joe in like he was one of their own. He and Shiloh were already planning a short retreat to Tallahassee as soon as they could get away.

Jake released my hand long enough for me to give Joe a quick hug, then grasped it again as we made our way to a pew near the back. Behind us I heard Karen murmur something to Joe.

The service was short: a couple songs, a prayer from the pastor of the Fowlers' church, a few words from Joe, and then we were filing back out.

No one seemed inclined to linger.

Karen dropped Jake and me off in front of Lighthouse Coffee with a promise to call later, and the two of us went in and sat at our usual table.

We drank our coffee in a companionable silence, watching the tourists flow through the store and listening to the hum of activity from Southern Treasures. Occasionally we heard a squawk from Bluebeard as he entertained the customers.

I thought about Julie's note, the one I found when I finally got home from the sheriff's station. She'd known about Uncle Louis almost as long as I had, and apparently he begged her for coffee when I wasn't around. He was incorrigible.

Jake set down his empty coffee cup and held out his hand to me. "Let's go upstairs and see how it's going," he said.

I let him help me up and we cleared the table, dropping our dishes in the kitchen on our way to the stairs.

Saturday meant no construction, and the upstairs seemed almost spacious without the crowd of workmen, tools, wires, pipes, and lumber.

There was still a lot to do, and there was still a pile of Pansy's boxes in the corner, but I could see my new apartment starting to take shape.

It was going to be a wonderful space.

And there was definitely enough room for two.

ABOUT THE AUTHOR

Christy Fifield writes the best-selling Haunted Souvenir Shop mystery series. As Christy Evans she also wrote the Lady Plumber mystery series. Under her real name of Christina F. York she writes romance, science fiction, fantasy, historical fiction, and nonfiction.

You can find her on Facebook (Christina.York.37), Twitter (ChristinaFYork), and Instagram (Christina.York.37) as well as through her website, YorkWriters.com, and on Patreon (TsunamiZone).

ALSO BY CHRISTY FIFIELD

Murder Buys a T-Shirt

Murder Hooks a Mermaid

Murder Sends a Postcard

Murder Ties the Knot

Writing as Christy Evans

Sink Trap

Lead Pipe Cinch

Drip Dead

Writing as Christina F. York

Romance

Dory Cove - Dream House - Loaves and Kisses

Intrigue

Alias: Strategic Reserve - Alias: A Touch of Death

Fantasy

Girls Gone Magic

Made in the USA
Middletown, DE
04 November 2022

14038617R00130